LEMONY SNICKET:

The
UNAUTHORIZED AUTOBIOGRAPHY

HARPERCOLLINS*PUBLISHERS*

Library of Congress Cataloging-in-Publication Data
Snicket, Lemony.
    Lemony Snicket : the unauthorized autobiography.
        p.   cm. — (Series of unfortunate events)
    Summary: The elusive author provides a glimpse into his mysterious and sometimes confusing life, using fanciful letters, diary entries, and other miscellaneous documents as well as photographs and illustrations.
    ISBN 0-06-000719-2 — ISBN 0-06-000720-6 (lib. bdg.)
    ISBN 0-06-056225-0 (pbk.)
    1. Snicket, Lemony—Juvenile fiction. [1. Snicket, Lemony—Fiction.   2. Humorous stories.]   I. Title.
PZ7.S6795 Lg   2002   2001051745
[Fic]—dc21   CIP
                                                                         AC

Arranged and rearranged by Alison Donalty and Robert Hult
❖

 INTRODUCTION

by

DANIEL HANDLER

AS THE OFFICIAL REPRESENTATIVE of Lemony Snicket in all legal, literary, and social matters, I am often asked difficult questions, even when I am in a hurry. Recently, the most common questions have been the following:

1. Will you please get out of my way?

2. Where did Lemony Snicket's *Lemony Snicket: The Unauthorized Autobiography* come from?

The replies to both of these questions are very long stories, so there is only room here to answer one of them. The origins of the *Unauthorized Autobiography* are somewhat cryptic—a word which here means "enigmatic"—but the story begins with a letter I received recently from the people who published this book.

Dear Mr. Handler, the letter began,

We have contacted you, Lemony Snicket's official representative in all legal, literary, and social matters, because of a rather enigmatic—a word which here means "mysterious"—matter which has captured our attention.

The story begins not too long ago at our offices. As you may recall, our offices are located in a tall, imposing building with a wide, imposing lobby and a middle-aged, imposing doorman, usually dressed in a coat that is too big for him, standing at the entrance to direct visitors to the elevators. On this particular day, the doorman on duty was a man who had been keeping a faithful diary for more than twenty-seven years, writing down every detail of his life with a ballpoint pen, and, when the pen ran out of ink and there was no stationery store nearby, a small piece of charcoal. The doorman had in fact taken this job in the lobby of the building containing our offices with the hope of getting his diary published as a book. Whenever people from the publishing house entered the building, the doorman would greet them with a smile and a handshake, and while he was shaking their hand he would slip a few pages from his diary into their hands, hoping that they would read the selection and change him from a doorman into an author.

One morning, I looked down at the crumpled and charcoal-stained pages that the doorman had given me, and one word caught my eye:

SNICKET

As you can imagine, all of us at the publishing house have been quite concerned about Lemony Snicket ever since his obituary appeared in *The Daily Punctilio*. Obviously, just because you read something printed on a page does not mean that it is true, but nevertheless we had been waiting for some word about Lemony Snicket and his work on the Baudelaire case, so I immediately uncrumpled the pages of the diary and read them as the elevator took me up to my office.

Dear Dairy, the diary began, the letter continued,

Today was a very cold and bitter day, as cold and bitter as a cup of hot chocolate, if the cup of hot chocolate had vinegar added to it and were placed in a refrigerator for several hours. Aside from the weather, however, the day was as normal as a group of seals with wings riding around on unicycles, assuming that you lived someplace where that was very normal, until a mysterious—a word which here means "arcane"—stranger came through the revolving door.

The stranger was a woman, at least as tall as a small chair and probably as old as someone who attended nursery school many years ago. She was entirely dressed in articles of clothing, and had nothing on her feet except a pair of socks and two shoes. She cast a desperate glance around the lobby of the building, which was as empty as a beehive when all of the bees have been driven out of it, and then thrust a packet of papers into my hands and began to speak in a voice that reminded me distinctly of her own.

She explained that the papers had been given to her by a stranger, who told her the following story:

One very cold day, not so long ago, an older gentleman of my acquaintance took me to supper at a club in a part of the city I had never known about. The older gentleman of my acquaintance had been a member of the club back when he lived in the city, and was always welcomed there whenever he visited. The club was located in an enormous, imposing mansion, painted green and decorated with a large, imposing insignia emblazoned on its door.

It will do me no good to describe the insignia— my writing skills are, in my humble opinion, simply terrible—so I will try to copy it here on this very page:

The dinner was quite delicious, and the older gentleman of my acquaintance seemed in the best of spirits, although every so often he gave me a small, secretive smile, as if he were keeping some arcane—a word which here means "abstruse"—secret that he was saving for dessert. Dessert, however, was not an arcane secret, but an arcane pudding.

After the pudding, the older gentleman of my acquaintance and I retired to an enormous, imposing living room to enjoy an after-dinner brandy, and the arcane smile returned to his face as a number of older gentlemen not of my acquaintance joined us, clearly for some sort of meeting. Not being a member of the club, I offered to leave, but the older gentleman of my acquaintance told me I might find the meeting of much interest, so I remained. Without any explanation, one of the older gentlemen not of my acquaintance took out a packet of yellowing parchment, all done up with string, from the folds of his overcoat. This packet was even less of my acquaintance than any of the gentlemen who were not of my acquaintance, and I moved my chair forward to get a better view so that I might become acquainted with it. The arcane smile left the man's face, and with some difficulty his fingers, attached to his hand, of course, undid the string, and after the gentleman cleared his throat and looked around briefly at the assembled company, he began to speak, although whether he was reading from the first page of the manuscript or merely talking to us I could not guess. He said:

Members of the club, honored guests, and any duchesses who might happen to be here in disguise:

I hesitate to tell you the story of how this packet of information concerning Mr.

SNICKET

came into my possession. It is well known that one of the easiest ways to avoid the attention of one's enemies is to concoct a long, false tale about how something was passed to you by a mysterious stranger, or how you received a letter out of the blue, or a message hidden in a handshake and written in illegible writing. So I will not tell you the following story:

My aunt, who is either a woman named Julie Blattberg or a woman whose name I am pretending is Julie Blattberg, gave me a small key that unlocked a box that contained a key which in turn unlocked another box that contained the information that makes up this book, and made me swear never to let it reach the public, even in the enormous, imposing living room of some abstruse—a word which here means "cryptic"—private club, among trusted associates enjoying after-dinner brandy . . .

That reminds me, the letter continued, I would like a brandy myself. Please excuse me for a moment.

Thank you. As I was saying, if I were to tell you that my aunt made me promise only to give this packet to my niece or nephew, except I don't have a niece or nephew and don't expect I shall ever have one, what with my brother's rash, I wouldn't expect you to believe it, so I will not give you any sort of introduction to this autobigraphy at all, except for these three statements:

1. This book does not appear to be a forgery, which is not to say that the story is true—only that it is accurate.

2. That this book comes from Mr. Snicket is unquestionable, which is not to say that some do not question it.

3. The book is more or less divided into thirteen sections, each with a question for a title. It is not known whether it was divided by Mr. Snicket or another party, although Mr. Snicket rarely attends parties. The thirteen questions are as follows:

CONTENTS

These are simply not the proper
questions: In the interest of
keeping the Baudelaire file as
accurate as possible and as focused
as feasible I have retitled each
of the thirteen chapters.

— LS

To My Kind Editor,

Please rewrite the editor's
note to read as follows:

The thirteen chapters of <u>The Unauthorize</u>
<u>Autobiography of Lemony Snicket</u> should n
be read at all.

— *LS*

Editor's note:

The thirteen chapters of Lemony Snicket: The Unauthorized Autobiography may be read in any order.

Another Editor's note:

Some of the photographs in this book were taken by Julie Blattberg.

To My Kind Editor,

Please rewrite another editor's note to read as follows:

Some of the photographs in this book were not taken by Julie Blattberg.

— LS

CHAPTER ONE

~~Why was Mr. Snicket's death published in the newspaper?~~

Who took this?

Obituaries

Lemony Snicket, Author and Fugitive

Lemony Snicket, author of A Series of Unfortunate Events, the purportedly true chronicles of the Baudelaire children, was reported dead today by anonymous and possibly unreliable sources. His age was given as "tall, with brown eyes." He leaves no known survivors.

Born on a cattle farm rather than in a hospital, Snicket had a promising scholarly career, beginning with a job as a theatrical critic—in all senses of the word—for this very newspaper, followed by the publication of several promising anthropomorphic treatises, a word which here means "very long reports." This period of professional contentment—and, allegedly, unrequited love—ended when news broke of his involvement with V.F.D. and the accompanying scandal was reported in these very pages.

Mr. Snicket became a fugitive from justice and was rarely seen in public, and then usually from the back. Several manhunts—and, due to a typographical error, womanhunts—proved fruitless. At last the Baudelaires' story, and his, appears to be over.

As no one seems to know when, where, how, and why he died, there will be no funeral services. A burial may be scheduled later this year.

4

NOTE TO FILE:

I have arrived early at the harbor and still have a few minutes before the *Prospero* is scheduled to appear, so I thought I might jot down a few notes concerning the news of my death, which was alarming but not true. I am, as of half-past four this afternoon, still alive, and was most certainly alive the day I sat at the Café Kafka with my afternoon tea and read my obituary in the newspaper.

The Daily Punctilio has never been a reliable newspaper: not when I worked there as part of an undercover assignment, not when that terrible reporter began to write about the Baudelaire case, and not when they advertised a sale on three-piece suits a few days ago, at a store that turned out to sell nothing but Indian rugs. Unlike a reliable newspaper, which bases its articles on facts, *The Daily Punctilio* bases its articles on innuendo, a word which here means "people who call up newspapers and tell them things that aren't necessarily true."

The only thing that turned out to be true about my obituary was the last sentence, and this morning I had the curious experience of attending my own burial. To my astonishment, quite a crowd showed up for the event—mostly people who had believed the earlier stories about me in *The Daily Punctilio,* and wanted to be sure that a notorious criminal was indeed dead. The crowd stood very quietly, seeming scarcely to move or even breathe, as if the news of their deaths had also been printed in the newspaper. I stood outside, shielding my face beneath an umbrella, as my coffin was carried into a long, black car, and the only sound I could hear was the mechanical *click!* of someone operating a camera.

Sometimes, when you are reading a book you are enjoying very much, you begin thinking so hard about the characters and the story that you might forget all about the author, even if he is in grave danger and would very much appreciate your help. The same thing can happen if you are looking at a photograph. You might think so hard about whatever is in the photograph that you forget all about the person behind the camera. Luckily, this did not happen to me, and I managed to take note of the person in the crowd who took the picture you probably have in this file. The photographer is standing in the seventh row of the crowd, twelfth from the left-hand side. As you can see, the person has hidden his or her camera behind the person standing eleventh from the left-hand side. That is why I am waiting here at this fogged-in harbor, in order to

The *Prospero* has arrived, so I will stop writing and file these notes with my letter, written so many years ago, to Professor Patton concerning inaccuracies regarding my birth. It makes me sad to think that my whole life, from the cradle to the grave, is full of errors, but at least that will not happen to the Baudelaires.

Dr. Charley Patton
Adjunct Professor, Folk Song Department
Scriabin Institute for Accuracy in Music

Dear Professor Patton,

It was with much relief that I received your letter concerning the folk ballad "The Little Snicket Lad." As you note, it is one of the most popular ballads of the region, and I have often heard it played in theaters, inns, and grocery stores whenever I am visiting, usually accompanied by an accordion. Though the tune is pleasant, the song is not an otherwise fair representation of my childhood, and I welcome the opportunity to correct at last the inaccuracies in the lyrics.

Please forgive the informality of my response—I have merely typed some brief notes to the lyrics you have sent me. I am preparing to be married at present, so I do not have time for the lengthy, scholarly report I usually write in cases like this.

The Little Snicket Lad

Verse One:

On a   charming   little cattle farm

Near   a   pretty deadly   lake,

Was a   ve - ry preg - n -   ant wo - ma - n,

And   her husband, known as Jake.

Though   they lived   in   a big mansion,

Down Robber Road   a   tad,

It wa - s   at the fa - rm the la - dy

Bore   the little Snicket   lad.

The first inaccuracy is in the very first line: I was not, nor have I ever been, born on a cattle farm. Thanks to "The Little Snicket Lad," the rumors of my birth have followed me all my life—I expect that someday my obituary will also claim I was born on a cattle farm. The place where I was born is not a cattle farm. As proof, I offer a photograph of the place, as seen from across the "pretty deadly" lake, which froze over in winter:

As you may be able to discern from the photograph, Valorous Farms Dairy has more than three hundred cows within its fences, but these animals only surrender their milk, not their lives. It may seem like a small difference, but not if you are a cow or a child, as I was, who not only was born on a dairy farm (simply because my parents stopped by to purchase garlic butter at exactly the wrong time) but also became friends with the cheesemakers who lived on the premises. These cheesemakers, whose names I will not reveal, remain very close associates ~drat!~ of my entire family. It is risky to divulge this information, even to a scholar such as yourself, but as part of my work with the heroes of this ballad, I often have to deliver secret information, which I sometimes hide in a letter beginning "Dear Dairy." If the letter is intercepted, it will be dismissed as cheesemaker correspondence, or mistaken for a fragment of a "Diary," spelled incorrectly.

The remaining errors in the first verse are quite minor. To say my father was "known as Jake" is not quite true—he was known as Jacob to everyone but his longtime bridge partner—and, as you can probably guess, the line about Robber Road is a fabrication. Robber Road is located clear across the county from my childhood home and Valorous Farms Dairy. I suspect the name "Robber Road" was chosen to emphasize the thieving nature of the chorus:

I have tried without success to look up the date of my departure in a good almanac but have been unable to verify that the moon was indeed "gray" that particular evening. An almanac is my only chance of verifying this claim, as I do not remember it myself. I was carried out of the kitchen by my ankles, as is the custom, so I was facing downward and could not see the sky, and the windows of the car were tinted, so absolutely everything looked gray to me as I was driven away from home.

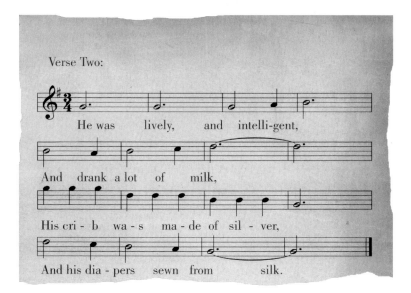

Verse Two:

He was lively, and intelli-gent,

And drank a lot of milk,

His cri - b wa - s ma - de of sil - ver,

And his dia - pers sewn from silk.

Both his siblings wat - ched him,

And his mother, and his dad,

But someone e - lse wa - s wat - ch - ing

O'er the little Snicket lad.

I may well have been an intelligent if not particularly lively child, and like all infants not cursed with severe allergies I did drink much milk, but the second half of the first half of the second verse is utter nonsense. My parents would never have indulged in silver cribs and silk diapers. Enclosed here is proof. This photograph was given to me in the automobile, as evidence that the passengers had indeed been "watching" me. I give it to you now.

The question that seems most important to me cannot ever be answered, I fear, as all of the people who would know are either dead, hiding somewhere, or enemies of mine. The question is "Who took this?" My mother asked the same question when she returned home that fateful day and found waiting for her not three young children but one worried husband and two half-full cups of tea.

Chorus:

And then they took him, yea they took him,

They took him far a - way,

They to - ok him in the de - ad of night,

Beneath a moon of gray.

They took him from the kitchen,

Like you'd take a midnight snack,

The V. F. D. the - y t - o - ok him,

And they never brought him back.

It has always bothered me that the song implies that I was taken while still in diapers. In fact, I have heard an alternate version of the ballad performed in the North, with the lyrics of the chorus as follows:

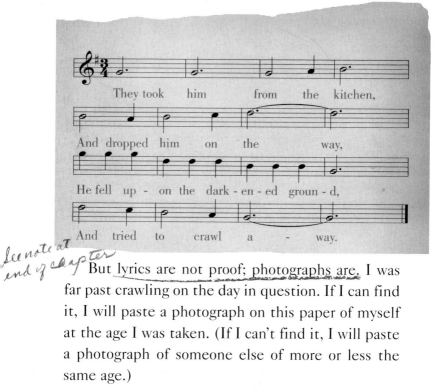

They took him from the kitchen,
And dropped him on the way,
He fell up - on the dark - en - ed groun - d,
And tried to crawl a - way.

See note at end of chapter

But lyrics are not proof; photographs are. I was far past crawling on the day in question. If I can find it, I will paste a photograph on this paper of myself at the age I was taken. (If I can't find it, I will paste a photograph of someone else of more or less the same age.)

On to Verse Three:

Verse Three:

One evening Jake was chopping wood,

And his wife was at the mill,

The sib - lings two we - re drin-k - ing tea,

And the house was very still.

They came in through the win - dows,

Not the door, which was the fad,

A long bla - ck car was par-ked out - side,

For the little Snicket lad.

17

This is more or less accurate, much to my mother's dismay, who always wished that she had delayed her investigation one more day, so she could have been at home that day to say good-bye. My brother insists that he was allowed to finish his tea before departure but this has been disputed over the years.

Chorus:

And then they took him, yea they took him,

They took him far a - way,

They to - ok him in the de - ad of night,

Beneath a moon of gray.

They took him from the kitchen,

Like you'd take a midnight snack,

The V. F. D. the - y t - o - ok him,

And they never brought him back.

It has just occurred to me that "never" might be too strong a word. An accurate version of the chorus would substitute the word "never" with the word "rarely," although that would scarcely be as dramatic.

Finally, there is the coda, a phrase which here means "verse at the end that you found so perplexing":

Coda:

"When we grab you by the ankles,
Where our mark is to be made,
You'll so-on be do-ing no-ble wor-k,
Although you won't be paid.

When we drive away in secret,
You'll be a vol-un-teer,
So do-n't scre-am wh-en we take you:
The world is quiet here."

This is entirely accurate. The only thing I can think to add is that I can see no reason why the entire coda is in quotes.

I do hope you find these notes helpful in your own noble work.

With all due respect,

Lemony Snicket

Lemony Snicket

P.S. the musical score that you enclosed is completely incorrect—the tune appears to be a well-known hymn of naval disaster. If possible, I will record the correct music and send you a copy on cassette.

P.P.S. I don't think I can be of any help as to the other ballad you mentioned. I will check with K., but I don't remember anybody named "Old McDonald" at the Valorous Farms Dairy, and I don't think "E.I.E.I.O." refers to a secret organization of any kind.

" They took him from the kitchen
and dropped him on the way,
He fell upon the darkened ground,
and tried to crawl away. "

CHAPTER TWO

~~Why has Mr. Snicket
dedicated his life to
the Baudelaire case?~~

Is this letter authentic?

23

❄ ❄ ❄ ❄ ❄ ❄ ❄ ❄ ❄ ❄ ❄ ❄ ❄

Vivez l'esprit

My dear Mr. Snicket,

Thank heaven you are alive and relatively well! Last night, when I arrived at the Orion Observatory to give my annual lecture to the Meteorological Society, I saw someone breaking into a navy blue Jeep parked in the southwest corner of the parking lot, and my heart leaped: perhaps there was a chance you were still alive. I did not expect to find out for certain until the usher handed me your letter. You took a terrible chance in contacting me, but I am glad you did. I am so sorry that I was unable to prevent, or at least delay, your capture at my masked ball that evening, and I have been worried sick all these years that you were dead, despite rumors of your activities spreading through the network of loyal members. There are not many of us left, Mr. Snicket, but we are ready to help you in any way we can.

I cannot, however, help you answer the question you wrote me on that gum wrapper. That masked ball was the last public event the members of the organization dared attend together, so if one of them hid something in the guest room it would have been that evening, probably during the salad course, when Baron van de Wetering, costumed as an oak tree, created a distraction by pretending there was a tiger underneath the table. After the disastrous end to the evening, I did not dare call attention to your belongings which the police forgot to confiscate—they might have deduced that you were attending the party after all, and made things even worse for all of us.

O Mr. Snicket, everything you kept in my home is gone. Your bullfighting costume is gone, along with all of the other disguises you kept with me: the fake wooden leg, the box of wigs, and that strange suit that enabled you to look like a chest of drawers. Your typewriter is gone, and the bright blue accordion, which I believe you told me was your third favorite. Everything in that guest room is gone, and all the things in the guest room next door. Beatrice, of course, is far past complaining about lost possessions—the very reason, I am certain, that you have dedicated your life to researching the lives of those three poor children.

Are they gone, too? It seems everything is nowadays.

Gone are all my beloved snacks, and my furniture: the tables are gone, round, square, rectangular—all the tables, and the chairs that sat with them. Gone are the drapes, except for the fireproof ones, which still sit in a heap, awaiting the beginning of the trial. Gone is the grand staircase with those two carved wooden crows at the ends of each of the banisters. Gone are all of the houseplants, and the cloth napkins with the crest of Winnipeg embroidered on one side and the underground map of the city embroidered on the other. Gone are the wigs *I* used, when I wanted to disguise myself as you disguised as someone else. Gone is the cigar box my father gave me, on my first visit home after I was taken, and gone is my childhood bed, where my tutors at V.F.D. watched over me until it was time to grab me by my ankles and introduce me to my new life. Everything is gone, Mr. Snicket. Every page of every book in my private library—*Charlotte's Web, Green Mansions, Ivan Lachrymose: Lake Explorer*—is unreadable ash.

It was so cold that I closed my windows and could not hear the crickets, so it was the sound of a collapsing bookcase that woke me that night, and I hurried out of the blazing mansion into the snow, dressed in my pajamas and clutching a handful of photographs that I had been looking at before I fell asleep. I was gazing at these photographs and wondering how everything could have gone so wrong. It seems to me, my dear friend, that one moment you and I were becoming friends in the infirmary, telling each other stories to distract us from the pain in our ankles, and the next moment the entire organization was scattered, like ashes blowing in the woeful and watery Winnipeg winds. Fire is like greed, my comrade. It spreads across the world, thinking only of itself, seizing everything it sees, and ruining everyone's fun.

Take these photographs, Mr. Snicket. They are all I can offer you, besides my loyalty and concern and two handkerchiefs I have just now found in my pockets. Study these pictures, my friend—the portrait of your sister and me, the portrait we told everyone was your sister and me but really wasn't, the snapshot of the Second Annual Codebreaking Picnic, and these two images of our meeting hall, the first one empty and the second one with one lone figure, waiting patiently for the session to begin in that enormous room of green wood. How content that young woman looks, don't you think? How content, and yet how flammable.

With all due respect,

NOTE TO FILE:

This letter reached me here at Veblen Hall, where I am waiting to interview some of the caterers about who exactly was driving the car that terrible day. As moving as her words are, I cannot be sure this is really the Duchess of Winnipeg. The Jeep outside the Orion Observatory was of course not navy blue but black, and parked in the northwest corner, not the southwest. She would never forget this. The real R. was tested on this information every month for more than seven years. Is she trying to tell me something? Was there another Jeep parked in the lot? Or is this a letter from a liar? These photographs could have been stolen from her mansion the night of the party, or could have been manufactured somehow—perhaps by the advanced computer at Prufrock Preparatory School.

The letter was wrapped in a white linen napkin, with the crest of Winnipeg embroidered on one side. The other side is blank. Crickets are usually silent in winter. I fear the worst.

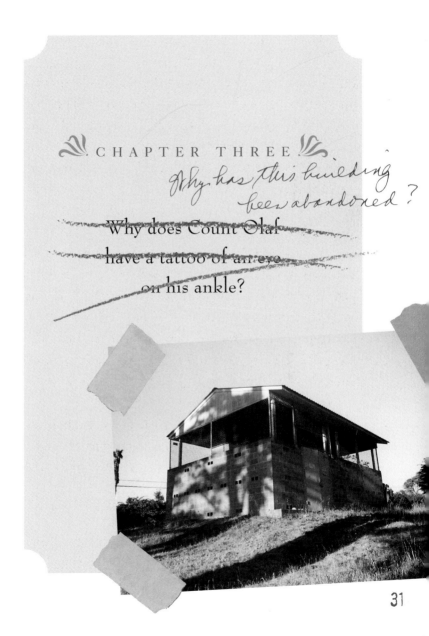

CHAPTER THREE

Why has this building been abandoned?

~~Why does Count Olaf have a tattoo of an eye on his ankle?~~

What follows is the transcript of the
meeting of the Building Committee of ▓▓▓
on April ▓▓ In attendance were J, L, M,
R, R, M, L, K, D, S, and I. Note: the
names of the attendees are given by the
first initial of their first name,
except for I, which is a pronoun. Some
people in attendance had the same first
initial, which makes this transcript
somewhat hard to follow, but no matter:
The Code of V.F.D. dictates that these
minutes are not to be read by anyone
who did not attend the meeting.

(sound of gavel banging)

M: I hereby call this meeting to order. Is the secretary ready to transcribe the minutes?

J: I am.

M: We will begin with roll call. Will the Vice Chancellor please read the committee list to see if anyone is missing?

R: I will. Please answer when I call your name. J?

J: Yes.

R: J?

J: Yes.

R: M?

M: Yes.

R: M?

M: Yes.

R: K?

K: Yes.

R: K?

K: I already said "Yes."

R: Sorry, I couldn't hear you. D?

D: Yes.

M: D, are you here representing L, or are you here as an independent agent?

L: I am here, so there is no reason for D to represent me.

R: Sorry, I didn't see you. L?

L: Yes.

R: L? Oh, I just spoke to you, L. Sorry. S?

S: **Yes.**

R: R?

R: Yes.

R: And R, **that's me.** Everyone is accounted for, **M.**

M: Very good. Let us begin by reciting the pledge.

J, L, M, R, R, M, L, K, D, S, J: The world is quiet here.

M: Very good. Now, before we get to the matter at hand, I have a few announcements. Tonight at seven P.M. we will meet in the lobby of the building two doors down from this one to proceed to the seven thirty P.M. showing of *Werewolves in the Rain*, directed by Dr. Sebald, in order to receive his coded message. Tomorrow morning at nine A.M. sharp will be the monthly examination for neophytes

R, L, K, B, J, E, and G, so our mapmaking session will be moved from the examination hall to the sculpture garden—

R: —which is much prettier anyway.

M: Well, yes. Which brings us to the urgent matter at hand.

L: What's the matter with your hand?

M: No, that's not what M meant, L. "At hand" is a phrase which here means "the matter we gathered to discuss." As you get older, these expressions will be easier to understand.

J: Please pass the brandy.

M: Please continue, M.

M: Thank you. I'm afraid that we're going to have to move our headquarters once more.

R: No!

D: It can't be! Not already!

M: I'm afraid it may already be too late,

D. Our spies at *The Daily Punctilio* tell us that G may be publishing our address in her "Secret Organizations You Should Know About" column.

J: But no one should know about **our** organization!

M: That's precisely M's point. We **must** switch locations one more time.

R: This is becoming absurd.

R: I agree. I'm nine years old, but I'm concerned that this kind of disruption will seriously affect our younger members.

R: R's right. We are entering people's homes—

J: We get permission first.

L: Let her finish.

R: I will finish. We are entering people's homes, taking young children who show exceptional observational and/or notetaking skills, and isolating them, for long periods at least, from people they know. We assign them to strangers and scatter them across the globe, performing errands that are per- plexing to them, until their ankles have healed, until we know they can be trusted, and until we know that no one is searching for them any longer. Then, finally, we bring them to headquarters so they can learn the skills they need before they are introduced back into society, in order to make sure the world remains, as we say, quiet.

K: And extinguished.

R: But if we further disrupt the training process, we risk confusing our neophytes even more. Tomorrow morning, for instance, are our monthly examinations. If these young people are up all night, helping us move all of the novels, sleeping bags, decanters, cameras, files, disguise kits, maps, coffee grinders, blueprints, code-books, fishing rods, notebooks, false menus, briefcases, corkscrews, bird guides, office supplies, goldfish bowls, false maps, garden hoses, magnifying glasses, musical instruments, nets, electrical cords, jewelry, toolboxes, spectroscopes, projectors, pet food, heavy winter coats, playing cards, curtains, caviar spoons, lockpicks, ropes, folding tables and ottomans, dictionaries and atlases, cages, chopsticks, bicycles, grappling hooks, sailing equipment, tin cans, storage tanks, false address books, false blueprints, telegraph devices, smoke canisters, building facades, false coffee grinders, disguise kits—

J: You already said "disguise kits."

R: If they stay up all night bringing

all of this material to a new head-quarters—assuming we can find one—how do you think they will perform on the exams? As we know from S's report on Prufrock Preparatory School, if young people do not get enough sleep, their work is likely to suffer. Someone might, for example, forget crucial information regarding the exact location of the automobiles we use to store necessary files and convey messages, or they could forget the Sebald Code and think there were eight uncoded words between each coded word, instead of ten. The sugar bowl secret could slip their minds entirely. This could lead to grave misunderstandings during coded communication, and we can't afford that.

M: Neither can we afford to be discovered. If our location is revealed in *The Daily Punctilio*, the building will likely be destroyed by the end of the week.

41

J: But how did that terrible reporter discover our location? We stopped inscribing the insignia on the outside of our buildings a very long time ago, and we haven't used green wood as construction material for quite some time.

M: There's no time to find out how we were found out.

J: On the contrary, M. It is almost too late to find out how the reporter found us out. It is time that we said here in an official meeting what we've been saying quietly to one another for quite some time: an enemy has infiltrated our ranks.

K: Infiltrated?

J: "Infiltrated" is a word which **here** means "snuck in without our noticing."

K: I *know* what the word means. When I said "infiltrated?" I meant "Do you really think so? That can't be so."

R: K is right.

R: No, J is.

R: K.

R: J.

R: K.

R: J.

R: K!

R: J!

M: Enough! We can discuss this at another time.

J: I'm sorry, M, but we should discuss this now. Since I have joined the organization, we have been forced to flee from a total of seven headquarters. I first met all of you—except for L, of course—at 1485 Columbia Road, which we had to abandon almost immediately in favor of that brick building with the scraggly hedges. Two months later we spotted someone taking photographs while one of our agents, and two total strangers, were walking outside, so we had to move everything over to that building with the two round towers, in a neighborhood so foggy that all of our sunflowers died and we had to discontinue that particular experiment. Then M woke us up in the middle of the afternoon in order to abandon the foggy building for new headquarters hidden in the Versailles Post Office, only to flee to a rival post office a year later. From then on we decided to go underground, beginning with the network of tunnels we had to dig beneath that lamppost, but our spies at *The Daily Punctilio* advised us to dig a new headquarters, underneath the "abandoned shack" in the northwest region of the

Finite Forest. Who knows how much information and equipment we have lost, packing and unpacking so many times? Who knows what precious time is gone forever? There is only one explanation for why our secret location has been discovered, over and over again: a member of V.F.D.—perhaps even someone in this very room—has betrayed us.

E: (laughs)

O: Indeed, ladies and gentlemen, perhaps someone in this very room has betrayed you!

M: O!

K: And E! We didn't see you there behind the puppet theater.

M: E and O, neither of you are welcome at this meeting.

O: Actually, I prefer to be called T.

M: We're not going to call you anything at all. Please leave at once.

E: We're not going anywhere, you fools.

O: Take a look at this!

(gasps from quite a few people)

L: Egad!

M: Put that back in its box immediately!

O: Not until I issue the following demands:

As instructed, this transcript will be stored in separate halves. The first half concludes here, and will remain in my files, along with the accompanying photographs and a report on a possible neophyte. The second half will be hidden between pages 302 and 303 in a copy of *Ivan Lachrymose: Lake Explorer*, a very tedious biography it is unlikely anyone will read. That book will be hidden under someone's bed.

Easy to reach window
from top of tree

1485 Columbia Road

1485 Columbia Road ?

48

Total strangers

OCT 72

W? H? O?

A.

VERSAILLES POST OFFICE

B.

Let's dig here.

50

Who knows how much
information and
equipment we have
lost, packing and
unpacking so many
times?

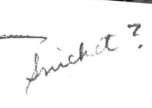

Snichot ?

51

Dear J,

Enclosed are some photographs of the neophyte we discussed earlier. It is getting more and more difficult to lurk in playgrounds nowadays, taking photographs without anyone's knowledge, but I nevertheless managed to acquire these three shots. As you can see, the subject seems physically adept enough, and has an admirable desire to protect himself against possible fire. As soon as I can verify which city he is in, I will be able to provide more information concerning possible recruitment ("taking").

CHAPTER FOUR

Where are the

Quagmire Triplets now?

Who is the
Tallest person in
this photograph?

From the desk of Lemony Snicket

Dear Dairy,

Dr. Sebald has not arrived for our appointment, and I am beginning to worry. As I'm sure you know, my dear cheesemakers, if you are expecting someone at a certain time and they have not shown up, it is difficult to know exactly when to give up and decide they are not coming. For instance, if you are a dentist and your patient has an appointment at five, at five twenty-five you might wait five more minutes before giving up and deciding that the patient has forgotten about the appointment, or is so frightened of having their teeth cleaned that they have locked themselves into a closet and refused to come out. If you are a birdwatcher and at six forty-five you are still waiting for the arrival of the six thirty pigeon, you might wait twenty more minutes before giving up and deciding that the pigeon has been eaten by a cat, or has accidentally overslept. But I am neither a dentist waiting for a patient nor a birdwatcher waiting for a pigeon, although I have both a bottle of mouthwash and a pair of binoculars with me at the moment. I am a researcher waiting for a film director, and I have been waiting for nineteen hours. I have decided to wait twenty more minutes before giving up and deciding that another member of V.F.D. has been captured by our sneaky, greedy, and moody enemies.

It is possible, of course, that Dr. Sebald is not captured, but merely delayed, and if that were the case he would have sent me a message in code. If I were in a theater, watching one of Dr. Sebald's movies, and the dialogue went as follows:

CHARACTER 1

(ringing a bell) I love eating prunes. They're so squishy, chewy, and delicious. I am always happy when I eat yummy prunes, unless they get trapped between my teeth.

CHARACTER 2

(nodding in agreement) Me too. When that happens I must send for my husband, who can usually—if he's not busy—help get them unstuck.

CHARACTER 1

(taking out a notebook and pen) Where does your husband live?

CHARACTER 2

With me, at Chewy Gum Lane, across from that prune museum we visited once.

(The two characters ring a bell again.)

then I would know that Dr. Sebald was trapped, and that I should send help at once. But instead I am sitting in this rowboat, staring out at the waters of the Swarthy Swamp and wondering where in the world he can be.

If he has been captured, then it is no longer safe for me to keep the pages from the script of his movie *Zombies in the Snow*. I was to return these pages to him nineteen hours ago—now that I am convinced that Dr. Montgomery never learned the Sebald Code—but if the filmmaker does not arrive in nineteen more minutes, I will enclose them with this letter. Please, my cheesemaking friends, hide these pages well.

Remember, you are my second-to-last hope that

the tales of the Baudelaire orphans can finally be told to the general public.

With all due respect,

Lemony Snicket

Lemony Snicket

P.S. To amuse myself during this nineteen-hour wait, I have written down several possible titles for a book about my own life. I do not expect that I will ever write such a book, but perhaps someday someone will, and you can provide them with this information if they ask for it. *or steal it ...*

LEMONY SNICKET:
Baudelaire Biographer

LEMONY SNICKET:
A Coward and a Gentleman

LEMONY SNICKET:
The Truth Behind the Man

LEMONY SNICKET:
The Man Behind the Truth

LEMONY SNICKET:
The Man Behind the Hedges

LEMONY SNICKET:
The Truth Behind the Lies

LEMONY SNICKET:
The Truth Behind the Lies Behind the Truth

LEMONY SNICKET:
The Truth Behind the Lies Behind the Truth
Behind the Man Behind the Hedges

LEMONY SNICKET:
The Truth Behind the Story Behind the Organization
Behind a Great Deal of Trouble

LEMONY SNICKET:
The Truth Behind the Man Behind the
Story Behind the Orphans

LEMONY SNICKET:
The Story of a Man Who Has Never
Burned Anything Down

LEMONY SNICKET:
The Story of a Man Who Has Never Burned
Anything Down, Despite What You May Have Heard

LEMONY SNICKET:
The Story of a Man Who Suspects Others of Having
Burned Things Down, Even Though He Himself Did Not

LEMONY SNICKET:
The Story of a Man Who Wishes Things
Had Turned Out Differently

LEMONY SNICKET:
The Story of a Man Who Needs Your Help

LEMONY SNICKET:
The Story of a Man Who Needs Your Help, Please

LEMONY SNICKET:
The Story of a Man, a Woman, and an Organization

LEMONY SNICKET:
The Story of a Man, a Woman, and Several Matches

LEMONY SNICKET:
The Story of a Man, a Woman, and Another Man

LEMONY SNICKET:
The Story of Three People, Two of Whom Are Male

LEMONY SNICKET:
The Story of Three Initials, All of Which Are Secret

LEMONY SNICKET:
The Story of Three Initials, All of Which Are Consonants

LEMONY SNICKET:
The Story of Three Siblings,
At Least One of Whom Is Dead

DO YOU SMELL SMOKE?
The Story of Lemony Snicket

LEMONY SNICKET:
A Good Man in Bad Trouble, Not Vice Versa

Screenplay for *Zombies in the Snow* by Dr. Gustav Sebald, pages 98–102.

DOLORES

(concluding her song)
I am very, very vexed,
Who knows who they'll eat next?

TOWN FATHER #1

(ringing a bell) Attention townsfolk! Evening is quickly approaching! Soon the sun will be hidden from view, and soon hundreds of hungry zombies will be in our beloved village! We must hide behind the barrier that the town fathers have constructed from sturdy oak. Stop building that snowman, Young Rölf, and get behind the oak barrier before it is too late!

YOUNG RÖLF

I'm not scared of zombies! I wanna build a snowman!

TOWN FATHER #2

Young Rölf, if you want to be a zombie survivor, you'll follow our orders!

YOUNG RÖLF

Bug off!

TOWN FATHER #1

We're sick and tired of your nonsense, Young Rölf. If you really don't care if the zombies eat you, then go make your snowman. By Apollo's fire, I wash my hands of this disobedient boy. He will meet his Maker by early evening. Come, my fellow townsfolk, let us hide behind our sturdy oak barrier. No zombies will get in to eat us, I promise you.

VILLAGERS

(cheering) Hear hear!

GERTA

(stepping forward) Hear hear? The town fathers tell you to abandon this little boy? The town fathers leave Rölf to die, and you say 'hear hear'? Where is your conscience? Where is your concern for young people? This town should be ashamed of itself!

TOWN FATHER #1

Stop talking like a film star, Gerta.

TOWN FATHER #2

Yes, you foolish milkmaid. Zombies approach, and arguing takes too much time when we should be in a safe place, like behind a sturdy oak barrier.

TOWN FATHER #1

Join us, Gerta. And bring Young Rölf. Otherwise you'll surely end up as one of the latest victims of hungry zombies.

GERTA

I have told you this three hundred times—zombies don't want to hurt us, or our children. My plan is to make friends with these zombies, and—

TOWN FATHER #2

Your plan is utter nonsense, Gerta. Zombies see us as fresh new meals, not potential friends!

YOUNG RÖLF

Ignore them, Gerta. You can be assistant snowbuilder.

TOWN FATHER #1

(leading the villagers off camera) You'll regret it, Gerta.

VILLAGERS

(as they leave) Hear hear!

GERTA

Oh, Rölf. Woe is me. I warned my fellow townsfolk that the barrier would not withstand the teeth of the zombies. They already ate through one wall of sturdy oak.

YOUNG RÖLF

That's why I'm staying here. Barriers of wood are no use.

(There is an enormous smashing sound, and several villagers run back into view of the camera.)

TOWN FATHER #1

Zombies! Zombies! Zombies! Zombies! Somebody save us!

TOWN FATHER #2

Help! Help! Help! Help! Help! Help! Help! Help! Help! Help! Beware!

(An alarm bell sounds.)

DOLORES

(beginning a song)
They'll eat my feet,
they'll eat my head,
I'm just a meal
for the walking dead.

EXECUTRIX OF THE SEBALD ESTATE

SALLY SEBALD

Dear Mr. Snicket,

What a relief it was to learn that you are alive and that Dr. Orwell is dead! For years I suspected the opposite, and assumed that one of your siblings was handling your affairs, as I am handling Gustav's. Siblings must take care of one another when they are all alone in the world, and it has been an honor to look after the Sebald papers. My brother was one of the most important film-makers of all time, and yet one never reads about him in history books or movie magazines. I hope that the books you are writing about the Baudelaires will make people remember the director of *Ghosts in the Desert, Goblins in the Garden, Mummies in the Jungle, Lions in the Mountains, Vampires in the Retirement Community, Leeches in the Lake, Werewolves in the Rain, Surgeons in the Theater, Gorillas in the Fog, Bats in the Train Station, Ants in the Fruit Salad, Zombies in the Snow, Hypnotists in the Office, Bigfoot in the Mall, Alligators in the Sewer, Realtors in the Cave, The Littlest Elf,* etc.

As you requested, I am sending you all of the photographs I can find in my brother's files for *Zombies in the Snow*. Gustav was quite particular when directing his films, because if any of the actors changed even one of the words in his script, the agents of V.F.D. who were hiding in the cinema audience might receive the wrong message. A crucial scene in *Zombies in the Snow*— beginning and ending, as always with the Sebald Code, with the ringing of a bell—was meant to deliver a message concerning the survivor mentioned in your letter, but my brother told me no more than this. Perhaps the enclosed photographs can provide you more information. The photographs are as follows:

1. Three actors from *Zombies in the Snow* posing in front of the snowman Gustav built specifically for this scene. In the center is the actor who played Young Rölf, whose name escapes me— Omar, maybe?

2. A photograph from the forest scene. Notice that Gustav had to use ceramic deer, instead of real ones, due to budget problems.

3. A photograph from the sled chase scene.

4. A photograph from the scene in which the towns-people try to stab the zombies with icicles growing on the fishing cannery.

5. Another photograph of the snowman, which Gustav left standing for several days after he was done filming the movie, before realizing that his message had not been received.

6. I am confused as to why this photograph is in the files of *Zombies in the Snow*. These three children—who appear to be siblings of about the same age—are not actors from the film, at least as far as I know. Note the notes.

?

sent to Prufrock
Preparatory School

7. A very rare photograph of Gustav Sebald himself, beginning work on the snowman.

I do hope you find this information helpful. Please do not hesitate to contact me again if there is any more assistance I can provide.

"The world is quiet here."

Yours, *Sally*

Sally Sebald

CHAPTER FIVE

~~Who~~
~~is~~
~~Beatrice?~~

Why was this actress replaced after only three performances?

NOTE TO FILE:

The following papers were found blowing together in the Financial District of the city.

Dear Dairy,

The archives of *The Daily Punctilio*—a phrase which here means "every single issue of a particular newspaper, gathered into a large collection"—have been destroyed. Perhaps it was foolish to keep this collection in plain sight, instead of locked up tight, but even the most secure collections of information—the Library of Records at Heimlich Hospital, which was kept behind a locked door, or Dr. Montgomery's books, which were guarded by watchful reptiles—are gone now, so perhaps it made no difference that the archives of *The Daily Punctilio* were merely stacked in large towers along a street in a small town near the Finite Forest. Our enemies would have found those crucial newspapers no matter where they were hidden, and destroyed them. Whenever I walk along the streets of this city, I grab whatever newspapers are blowing around on the sidewalks, just in case important files from the archive were not destroyed after all, and have blown all the way back to the city. I must be a ridiculous sight—a grown woman wading into the Fountain of Victorious Finance just to retrieve a scrap of newspaper—but it's my only chance of clearing the name of Lemony Snicket, if indeed he is still alive.

So far, the right papers have eluded me. The closest I have come is finding these articles, which appeared in the Theater Section over the course of that long and terrible week. I send them to you, my dear cheesemakers, so that you might put them with the rest of my brother's papers.

"The world is quiet here."

A Night at the Theatre

by our dramatic critic, Lemony Snicket

Even after more than a year writing theatrical reviews for this publication, there are many things I do not understand. I do not understand how Inspector Auster knew that the taxi driver was lying in last season's production of *The Case of the Vegetarian Murderer,* or why there was a tap-dance number in the middle of *Look Out for That Axe!* I do not understand why the Nancarrow Theater allows the audience to bring live sheep into the theater, but only on Saturday nights, or why a play about singing cats was allowed to be performed at all. I do not understand why Shirley T. Sinoit-Pecér won the Brooks-Gish Award for Best Actress even though some people suspected she was actually an *actor,* and I do not understand why some people attend the theater when it appears they would prefer to be

unwrapping candy or talking on the phone, and I do not understand why I should be expected to applaud for a bunch of skinny dancers just because they can stand on tiptoe longer than I can.

And now there is something else I do not understand. I do not understand why there have been so many changes to the play performed at the Ned H. Rirger Theater. As my faithful readers will recall, last week I reviewed the Rirger's performance of a play entitled *The World Is Quiet Here,* by the unknown playwright Linda Rhaldeen. In this very column I stated, "*The World Is Quiet Here* is the most important play of the season, and whether you are someone attending the theater for enjoyment or someone attending the theater to receive important coded information, you're sure to have a delightful and/or productive evening." I regret to say that I must take back every word of that praise after viewing last night's production.

For one thing, an announcement in the new production reveals that the name of the playwright was some sort of typographical error, and that the play is actually the work of Al Funcoot. My faithful readers will recall that I have not enjoyed Mr. Funcoot's previous efforts. I called his first play, *The Most Handsome Man in the World,* "a tedious, arrogant show," and referred to its sequel, *Why, I Believe I've Become Even More Handsome!* as "just another excuse for the play's one-eyebrowed star to show off." In addition, the title of the play has been changed from the noble, significant *The World Is Quiet Here* to the vaguely threatening *One Last Warning to Those Who Try to Stand in My Way.* At least, that is what I *think* the title is—the changes appear in the program in charcoal, and some of the words are difficult to read.

One Last Warning to Those Who Try to Stand in My Way

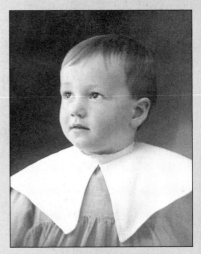

now bills itself as a "comedy," but this critic is not laughing. Gone is the crucial opening number, "Let the Bell Ring," and in its place is an annoying ditty entitled "Introducing a Very Handsome Man." The two actresses playing the Defenders of Liberty now have their faces painted a ghastly white color, and the part of the Little Sebald Lad, once played by the young actor pictured here, has been replaced by a sinister-looking person far too old for the part (also pictured here). But the most dispiriting replacement is that of the lead actress. My

the theater in disgust. Comedy, indeed—*One Last Warning to Those Who Try to Stand in My Way* feels more like a dastardly plot.

I only hope that this review is read by the general public before it is too late to escape, or have your ticket money refunded.

faithful readers realize that I am somewhat prejudiced in this case, as I am engaged to be married to the original actress, but last night's performance by Esmé (?—her last name was smudged in the program) was simply dreadful. This Esmé cannot act. She cannot sing. And she cannot whistle Mozart's Fourteenth Symphony, as the play—the original play, that is, *The World Is Quiet Here*—requires. By the time Esmé led the entire cast in the final number ("Place All Your Valuables on the Stage or Something Dreadful Might Happen to You"), I left

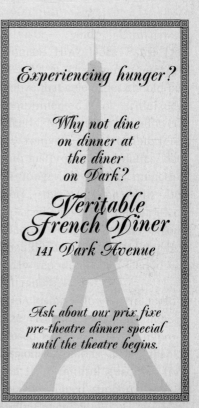

AN ANNOUNCEMENT

by our
Editor-in-Chief, Eleanora Poe

Due to his outlandishly rude opinions in yesterday's column, our dramatic critic Lemony Snicket has been fired. I myself, the Editor-in-Chief of *The Daily Punctilio,* recently attended a performance of Al Funcoot's *One Last Warning to Those Who Try to Stand in My Way,* starring Esmé (?—her last name was smudged in the program), and had a wonderful time. From the opening number, in which a handsome man introduced himself to the audience, I was utterly enraptured, and by the end of the evening I was having so much fun that I threw my purse and jewelry onto the stage.

In order to apologize to the star of the show, we will write nothing but nice things about her from now on, including a special article in tomorrow's edition entitled: "Actress, Financial Advisor, and Unmarried Woman: How Does Esmé Do It?" We at *The Daily Punctilio* realize that celebrities should be complimented, not criticized. Clearly, Mr. Snicket has allowed his romantic life to interfere with his professional duties, but no longer. Effective immediately, this column will be replaced with a new one entitled "Secret Organizations You Should Know About," written by a new reporter named Geraldine Julienne.

In closing, allow me to apologize for any inconvenience caused by Mr. Snicket's unprofessional opinions, and to thank you, my faithful readers, for your continued support of *The Daily Punctilio.*

A Night at the Theatre

by our dramatic critic, Lemony Snicket

As my faithful readers know, I have been fired from my job as dramatic critic for this newspaper, supposedly due to my negative opinions concerning Al Funcoot's dreadful play *One Last Warning to Those Who Try to Stand in My Way* and its lead actress, an extremely untalented and unpleasant woman named Esmé. I think it is only fair to inform you, my faithful readers, as to the real reason I have been dismissed. Eleanora Poe, the Editor-in-Chief of this paper,

AN ANNOUNCEMENT

by our
Editor-in-Chief, Eleanora Poe

I feel I must once again discipline our former dramatic critic, Mr. Lemony Snicket, who attempted to place one more column in this morning's *Daily Punctilio*. I'm sure that faithful readers of our glorious newspaper are not interested in reading critical comments about very talented actresses and playwrights. That is not a critic's job, which is why Mr. Snicket no longer has one.

From now on, we are keeping the doors to the printing press locked tight when they are not in use.

In closing, allow me to apologize one more time for any inconvenience caused my Mr. Snicket's unprofessional opinions, and to thank you, my faithful readers, for your continued support of *The Daily Punctilio*.

Watch for
Geraldine Julienne's column,
"Secret Organizations You Should Know About,"
beginning tomorrow!

❊ ❊ ❊ ❊ ❊ ❊ ❊ ❊ ❊ ❊ ❊ ❊ ❊

Vivez l'esprit

K—

I do not think it is safe for me to keep these two letters any longer, and for reasons I do not need to explain, it is impossible for me to write to Mr. Snicket. Will you please get these letters to a safe place—perhaps with Ike, or at that dairy farm you once told me about? I hope—as we all do—that someday these papers will save at least three lives.

If you do me this favor I will never forget, any more than I would forget the location of our secret Jeep, or the Sebald Code.

The Vineyard of Fragrant Drapes

Dear Mr. Snicket,

Congratulations on your upcoming marriage! We at the Vineyard of Fragrant Drapes are overjoyed to learn that your future includes wedding bells ringing.

Hello. Enclosed is an award-winning photograph of our beautiful wedding gazebo. If you prefer, the gazebo can be painted a different color. You or your future bride simply need to inform us—we are entirely at your disposal. White paint makes the place come alive, in our opinion, but we'll repaint the building if you do not think so.

The food, as you specifically requested, will not be from the Anxious Clown or Café Salmonella but will come from another fine restaurant nearby that specializes in tea parties. Here at the Vineyard we want to please our customers, so the sugar bowls will all be in place, we promise you. We'll count them if necessary.

Besides the gazebo and the catering, we will provide the following wedding accessories free of charge: candles to burn during the ceremony, three flower arrangements, an official wedding certificate you will probably want to frame for display in your home, and the enclosed souvenir—a photograph of our lovely grounds, inscribed "Beatrice and Lemony: Love Conquers Nearly Everything." The weather promises to stay beautiful during the entire week. You'll be sad to go away.

Ring, ring, ring, those wedding bells!

With all due respect,

The Vineyard

Beatrice and Lemony:
Love Conquers
Nearly Everything

The
Vineyard
of Fragrant Grapes

Dear Mr. Squalor,

Congratulations on your upcoming marriage! We at the Vineyard of Fragrant Grapes are overjoyed to learn that your future includes wedding ceremonies.

Enclosed is an award-winning photograph of our beautiful wedding gazebo, which is painted white. White paint makes the place looks fantastic, in our opinion.

The food, as you specifically requested, will come from Café Salmonella. We regret that we will be unable to provide sugar bowls, as your fiancée Esmé requested in a separate letter. Here at the Vineyard we want to please our customers, but some things are simply impossible.

Besides the gazebo and the catering, we will provide the following wedding accessories free of charge: candles to light during the ceremony, three flower arrangements, an official wedding certificate you will probably want to frame for display in the penthouse apartment we have heard you recently purchased, and the enclosed souvenir—a photograph of our lovely grounds, inscribed "Jerome and Esmé: Married After Only One Evening Together."

We cannot promise that the weather will remain beautiful during the entire week, of course, but we hope so.

With all due respect,

The Vineyard

Jerome and Esmé:
Married After Only
One Evening Together

CHAPTER SIX

What is V.I.D.?

Why did this ship leave three hours ahead of schedule?

THE DAILY PUNCTILIO

"All the News in Fits of Print"

TODAY'S PHOTO EXCLUSIVE:
SHIP DEPARTS EARLY!

Above: The *Prospero*, a ship that was scheduled to leave yesterday from Daedalus Dock at eight P.M. sharp, but instead left shortly before five o'clock for reasons unknown.

A man on the Black Rapids Deck attempted to explain to reporters from *The Daily Punctilio* why the ship was leaving early, but the only words audible over the sound of the ship were "Phase Two" and "Drat!"

Passengers holding tickets for the *Prospero* were left stranded on the ladder as the ship departed. "I do not intend to swim," exclaimed one passenger, who wished only to be identified as E.

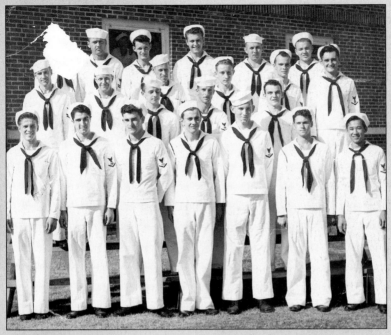

The Daily Punctilio has obtained this photograph of the sailors on board the *Prospero*. Is one of them responsible for the early departure? Front row, left to right: Sailor Gantos, Sailor Eager, Sailor Kerr, Sailor Whelan, Sailor Cleary, Sailor Snyder, Sailor Sones. Second row, left to right: Sailor Seibold, Sailor Walsh, Sailor Selznick, Sailor Creech, Sailor Danziger. Third row, left to right: Sailor Konigsburg, Sailor Lowry, Sailor Scieszka, Sailor Griffin. Back row, left to right: Sailor Snicket, Sailor Dahl, Sailor Woodson, Sailor Bellairs, Sailor Kalman, Sailor Peck.

Watch for tomorrow's Photo Exclusive:
BUS ARRIVES LATE!

O Brother,

I hope that this package reaches you safely, and that you are safe when it reaches you, and that I will be safe in making sure this package will reach you in safety, in a safe manner, and in a safe.

Your review of Funcoot's play has changed everything. O is more dastardly than we ever could have imagined, and it will no longer be possible for you to communicate with us through *The Daily Punctilio*. The organization has informed me that they will arrange for you to be fired, if possible. If it is not possible you will probably be fired anyway.

Inside the enclosed safe are the documents and required materials for Disguise Training, Phases One and Two. Under normal circumstances, new volunteers like ourselves would not receive disguise training until our years of apprenticeship were finished, but we have not been under normal circumstances for quite some time. For instance, currently I am under sixty feet of water, rather than under normal circumstances. Brother, you must run. You must run as you never have run before, at least as far as I know.

Once you have familiarized yourself with these

materials, disguise yourself as you see fit and travel via ferry to the town of Lake Lachrymose. There is a theme restaurant located on the main street called the Anxious Clown. The food is dreadful, but I'm afraid you'll have to eat there until you find a waiter who says to you the following sentence: "I didn't realize this was a sad occasion." That will indicate that he is one of us. You will reply, "The world is quiet here," and he will give you a letter containing instructions for leaving the country. Follow these instructions, and make sure you are not followed as you are following them.

We are all in terrible danger and thus must not communicate for a very long time. You must not write to D. You must not telephone K. You must not communicate with B at all, not even by telegram or carrier pigeon. I will try to communicate with B myself so that she does not believe all of the terrible things printed in *The Daily Punctilio*, but you must not risk her life along with your own.

I do not know when I will see you again. Someday, perhaps, the world will indeed be quiet once more, but until the fires have been extinguished we must go our separate ways and risk our separate lives. I feel, Lemony, as if we are drifting away from one another, as if one of us is on the ground and the other is in some wondrous device, floating away into the sky, like that self-sustaining hot-air mobile home H is always talking about building. I hope you are able to return home someday, Brother.

With all due respect,

Jacques

Jacques

P.S. The combination to the safe is a three-digit number, identical to the address of our headquarters on Dark Avenue.

DISGUISE TRAINING

PHASE ONE:
VEILED FACIAL DISGUISES

REQUIRED MATERIALS: FACE

OPTIONAL MATERIALS: HAT

Though "disguise" is a word which commonly means "a change of clothing to hide one's identity," it is not always necessary to alter what you are wearing in order to alter what you look like. Observe the photographs on the next page. At first glance, they look like photographs of twelve different people. If you examine the photographs closely, however, you will realize they are actually twelve different photographs of the same person, who has merely changed aspects of his face (smiling, frowning, facing different directions, etc.). If you are trying to fool a farsighted or dimwitted person, a veiled facial disguise might be enough.

Check yourself carefully to make sure you have all of the required materials listed above, as well as the optional materials if needed.

Try some of your own. You will be tested.

"The world is quiet here."

DISGUISE TRAINING

PHASE TWO:
VARIOUS FINERY DISGUISES

REQUIRED MATERIALS: V.F.D. DISGUISE KIT,
CONTAINING THE FOLLOWING ITEMS:

blazer (turquoise)
boots (black)
bouquet of flowers
bridal gown
business cards, to keep in purse, wallet, or pocket
cane (jeweled, turns into sword)
cane (regular)
cape (scarlet, silk)
charcoal
coat (blue, with badge)
coat (doorman's oversized)
coat (long, dark)
coat (medical)
coat (medium-length, beige)
coat (rain)

detective's badge

eyepatch

gloves

hands (fake)

hat (chef's)

hat (cowboy)

hat (doorman's)

hat (feathered)

hat (sailor)

hat (top)

helmet (motorcycle)

makeup kit, including lipstick and fake lipsticks,
   eyeshadow and glass eyes, eyebrow pencil
   and fake eyebrows, hairspray and haircoloring

mask (black, skinny)

mask (surgical)

money (to purchase additional disguises or snacks)

name tag, to put on chest

nameplate, to keep on desk

notebook

overalls

pants (sensible)

pants (silver)

photographs of false family members, to keep
   in purse, wallet, or pocket

pots
razor (to shave head, legs, and/or eyebrows)
robe (black)
shoes (formal)
shoes (plastic)
shoes (running)
shoes (sensible)
stockings
suit (black)
suit (clown)
suit (pinstripe)
suit (sailor)
suit (salmon)
suit (sweat)
sunglasses
turban
veil
vest (embroidered with gold thread)
wooden leg
wig (blond, braided)
wig (gray, judicial)
wig (multicolored, clownish)
wig (white, curly)

OPTIONAL MATERIALS: SUGAR BOWL

"Desperate times call for desperate measures" is an aphorism which here means "sometimes you need to change more than your facial expression in order to create a workable disguise." The quoting of an aphorism, such as "It takes a village to raise a child," "No news is good news," and "Love conquers all," rarely indicates that something helpful is about to happen, which is why we provide our volunteers with a disguise kit in addition to helpful phrases of advice. Observe the photographs at right. At first glance, they look like photographs of two different people. If you examine the photographs carefully, however, you will realize they are actually the same person, who has merely changed aspects of her face and clothing. In the first photograph (A), the volunteer (B) is using her actual face and regular clothing, both of which could be recognized by her enemies. In the second photograph (C), the same volunteer (still B, but calling herself D), has dramatically altered herself using the V.F.D. disguise kit and is now completely unrecognizable, particularly with the older gentleman (D, but calling himself B) standing in front of her.

A.

C.

Check your disguise kit carefully to make sure it contains all of the required materials listed and the optional materials if needed. Some possible disguises, using combinations of the required materials, are listed alphabetically below.

Admiral Disguise: coat (rain) + business card

Barbequer Disguise: coat (rain) + hat (chef's)

Boat Captain Disguise: eyepatch + wooden leg + hat (sailor) + business card

Bride Disguise: bridal gown + bouquet of flowers + veil

Bullfighter Disguise: cape (scarlet, silk) + vest (embroidered with gold thread) + mask (black, skinny)

Chief of Police Disguise: coat (blue, with badge) + boots (black) + gloves + helmet (motorcycle) + motorcyle (purchased with money)

Detective Disguise: sunglasses + shoes (plastic) + detective's badge + pants (silver) + blazer (turquoise)

Doorman Disguise: hat (doorman's) + coat (doorman's oversized) + charcoal

Foreman Disguise: overalls + mask (surgical) + wig (white, curly) + pots (Note: this disguise also may be used as a Surgeon Disguise or Pot

Salesman With Allergies Disguise.)

Gym Teacher Disguise: suit (sweat) + shoes (running) + turban

Judge Disguise: robe (black) + wig (gray, judicial)

Lab Assistant Disguise: coat (long, dark) + razor (to shave head and eyebrows)

Nudist Disguise: nothing

Operagoer Disguise: hat (top) + suit (black) + shoes (formal) + money (to create the appearance of wealth)

Optometrist Disguise: coat (medical) + boots (black) + cane (jeweled, turns into sword) + wig (blond, braided)

Receptionist Disguise: makeup kit + shoes (sensible) + stockings + nameplate

Taxi Driver Disguise: photograph of new baby to show to passengers

Waiter Disguise: suit (clown or salmon) + wig (multicolored, clownish, if clown suit used) + name tag

Note: So far, our volunteers have not found a use for a medium-length beige coat.

Try some of your own. You will be tested.

"THE WORLD IS QUIET HERE."

Dear Sir,

If you are reading this letter it means you were able to contact the proper waiter at the Anxious Clown. I'm sorry you had to eat there. I hope you didn't order the Surprising Chicken Salad.

Enclosed is a blueprint of the *Prospero*, a ship we have arranged to smuggle you out of the country, and two tickets for passage. The first is an ordinary ticket, which you will give to the man collecting tickets at the Front Gate (A). When you present the first ticket, you should be disguised as a passenger. The second is the special encoded ticket, which you will give to me in the Main Bridge (B). When you present the second ticket, you should be disguised as a sailor. I will be disguised as Captain S., using the Various Finery Disguises from Phase Two of Disguise Training.

To get to the Main Bridge (B), you must walk through the White Jacket Lounge (C), the Redburn Ballroom (D), and the Typee Shuffleboard Court (E).

Do not walk through any of the decks, which include the Ringman Deck (F), the Black Guinea Deck (G), and the Black Rapids Deck (H). Our enemies will undoubtably be stationed there, disguised as passengers and/or seagulls, and if they spot you they will probably throw you overboard (I).

Once you reach me and present me with the second, encoded ticket, the ship will depart. Good luck, sir.

"The world is quiet here."

With all due respect,

Captain S.
(aka J)

P.S. Incidentally, I rather enjoyed your theatrical reviews in *The Daily Punctilio*, and I was sorry to hear you would no longer be writing them.

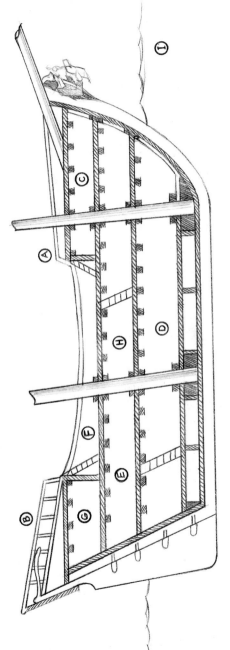

For true friends, old and new

Our latch string is hanging out

You're welcome here, so come inside,

THE
PROSPERO

Every Ship Has Its Own Fun!

All voyages aboard
The Prospero
depart from Daedalus Dock at
eight o'clock sharp.
Please arrive on time.
Latecomers will be forced to swim.

BOARDING PASS

This portion of the boarding pass should
be retained as evidence of your journey.

•••

Esta Porción del oase de abordar debe
guardarse como prueba de su viaje.

We've saved a place for you.

You'll be a volunteer,

When we drive away in secret,

So don't scream when we take you:

THE
PROSPERO

Every Ship Has Its Own Schedule.

All V.F.D. voyages aboard
The Prospero
depart from Daedalus Dock whenever
circumstances require.
Please arrive on time.
Latecomers will be forced to swim.

- -

BOARDING PASS

This portion of the boarding pass should
be retained as evidence of your journey.

· · ·

Esta Porción del oase de abordar debe
guardarse como prueba de su viaje.

The world is quiet here.

CHAPTER SEVEN

What has stained this man's jacket?

~~Why is there a secret passageway between the Baudelaire mansion and 667 Dark Avenue?~~

THE DAILY PUNCTILIO

"All the News in Fits of Print"

MURDER AT LUCKY SMELLS LUMBERMILL!

Lucky Smells Lumbermill, located in the small town of Paltryville, has been the site of a gruesome murder. Before detectives could arrive, a volunteer who wishes his identity to remain secret (see photo at right) arrived on the scene and investigated the matter thoroughly, reaching the conclusion that the person responsible was Count Olaf, along with a henchman experiencing hair loss whose name

A volunteer, examining logging equipment used in the murder.

THE DAILY PUNCTILIO

"All the News in Fits of Print"

ACCIDENT AT LUCKY SMELLS LUMBERMILL!

Detective Smith, Detective Jones, and Detective Smithjones, examining logging equipment used in the accident.

Lucky Smells Lumbermill, located in the small town of Paltryville, has been the site of a gruesome accident. Three detectives, who gladly gave their names to *The Daily Punctilio* (see photo at left), arrived on the scene immediately and investigated the matter thoroughly, reaching the conclusion that there was nobody responsible, since it was an accident. "Another case solved without any help from volunteers!" commented either Detective Smith or Jones, I forget which. "The only bad thing about this case, besides the death involved, is that I accidentally spilled coffee on my jacket."

Geraldine Julienne, reporter,
The Daily Punctilio

Dear Esmé,

My goodness!!! It was such a thrill to get a letter from an important person like yourself. Just think, not only are you the city's sixth most important financial advisor, but you're also a very famous actress, and you're writing to an unimportant reporter such as myself!!

As you know, the editor-in-chief of *The Daily Punctilio* just fired our dramatic critic, whose name escapes me (I've never been good with names but I still think I'm a pretty good reporter!!), so I'm confident you'll never get another bad review for your performances on the stage, whether you're acting in one of Al Funcoot's plays or something else.

Someday, I hope to uncover a major story—maybe a murder—but in the meantime, as you know, I just write a boring old column called "Secret Organizations You Should Know About." Sometimes, in order to make the column more exciting, I write rumors or things I make up, instead of facts. At your request, I'll tell you what was true in my column about 667 Dark Avenue, and what wasn't.

1. It is true that the penthouse to 667 Dark Avenue has recently been sold, to a Mr. Jerome Squalor.

2. It is true that Mr. Jerome Squalor is not married.

3. At your request, I did a little research about where you could find him. Every morning he has breakfast down the street at the Veritable French Diner, a very "in" restaurant. You should be able to find him there between seven thirty and eight thirty A.M., if you wanted to "accidentally" bump into him.

Good luck, Esmé! I'm so flattered that a talented and famous actress took the time to write me! If you ever need me to do anything—anything at all—please write again and I'll do it at once!

Your loyal fan,

Geraldine

Geraldine Julienne

P.S. You are the greatest!!!

Veritable French Diner
141 Dark Avenue

"Le Monde Ici, C'est Calme"

Breakfast Special

Raspberry scones—a phrase which here means "delicious pastries"—served with your choice of homemade butter and storebought jam, or vice versa. Accompanied by fresh-squeezed juice from the fruit, vegetable, or flower of your choice, along with coffee or tea, served with a small pitcher of milk and a sugar bowl.

Price: *As the aphorism says, "If you have to ask, you can't afford it."*

Lunch Special

A sandwich made exclusively from ingredients, served with your choice of a salad made exclusively from fresh things, or soup made exclusively from choice liquids. Accompanied by a beverage served in a glass, along with a small napkin and a sugar bowl.

Price: *Same as breakfast.*

Dinner Special

Chef's choice.

Price: *Slightly more than lunch.*

Dear Jerome,

I was alarmed to receive your wedding invitation and am writing you to say that under no circumstances should you marry that woman, at the Vineyard of Fragrant Drapes—I mean Grapes, of course—or anywhere else.

The reason you should not marry Esmé is the same reason I begged you to buy the penthouse apartment at 667 Dark Avenue and never, ever sell it, and the same reason people should never get tattoos. I cannot fully explain this reason for two reasons. The first reason I cannot explain this reason is that I made a solemn vow I would never tell anyone this reason. And the second reason I cannot explain this reason is that if you learned of this reason—or even the two reasons why I cannot explain this reason—that would be the reason that you would suddenly find yourself in danger. Even though I explain this reason for the two reasons I explained, I want to give you a reasonable explanation, so I will tell you everything I can.

I am not really a detective, my friend. I am a member of an organization that requires its members to pretend to be various occupations, including detective, ship captain, dramatic critic, duchess, waiter, and many others. For years this organization has behaved in ways that were as noble as they were secret, but recently this organization has experienced a schism, a word which here means "a member suddenly behaving in a greedy and violent manner and thus dividing the organization into two arguing groups." The member I am speaking of—I will just call him O, though currently he prefers S—has recently done a great deal of vicious, unfair, and impolite acts that I shudder to describe.

Perhaps you are wondering why you have not read about these vicious, unfair, and impolite acts in the newspaper, but I have reason to believe that O has somehow found a way to change the articles in *The Daily Punctilio* to avoid capture. For instance, a recent article described a deadly accident at Lucky Smells Lumbermill, solved by a detective who claimed to have spilled coffee on his jacket. But I, acting as a volunteer, arrived at the lumbermill before any detectives did, and I saw at once that the death was no accident.

A couplet I recently found, in the village where I am hiding, says it best:

Someone at the newspaper changed the story once again,

It was not coffee, but black ink, that made the jacket's stain.

Please, Jerome, do not marry this woman.

With all due respect,

Jacques

Jacques Snicket

Dear Jacques,

I was disappointed not to hear from you after I invited you
to my wedding. I even asked my doorman if he had mis-
placed any mail that had arrived during my honeymoon,
but he laughed at the very thought. Just in case, however,
I decided to write you again.

Esmé and I are happily married and living in the penthouse apartment you begged me to buy and never, ever
sell. Perhaps you can explain why if you come and visit
us. She says that she can't wait to meet you so she can
finally give you what you deserve. I assume she means a
present of some kind. I asked her to explain, but she grew
angry, and, as you know, I can't stand arguing.

I will give this letter to the doorman to make sure that
it will get to you. I would hate to lose touch with a friend
such as you.

Your pal,

Jerome

Jerome

P.S. We're thinking of adopting some children—do you
think that's a good idea? You know I always follow your
advice, my friend.

CHAPTER EIGHT

Why isn't Mr. Poe
as helpful as he ought to be?

Prufrock Preparatory School

"Memento ~~Mori~~ _Nero_":
Remember you ~~will die.~~ _the greatest violinist in the world_

Dear Mr. and Mrs. Spats,

Thank you very much for sending me the article that appeared in <u>The Daily Punctilio</u>. You were correct in making the assumption that I had not read about the danger of allowing young people to read certain books. The only section of <u>The Daily Punctilio</u> I read is the Music Section, in the hopes that there will be an article about the greatest violin player in the world (me).

Because of the article you sent me, I have fired Ms. K., the teacher who replaced Mr. Remora after he choked on a banana and decided to retire. Unlike Mr. Remora, Ms. K. was not interested in telling short stories while eating. Ms. K. preferred to have the children read books that I now know are entirely improper, thanks to Eleanora Poe, the honest and trustworthy Editor-in-Chief of <u>The Daily Punctilio,</u> and Geraldine Julienne, her star reporter. When I informed Ms. K. of my decision, she behaved exactly like any improper teacher and immediately kidnapped two children, holding them by the ankles as she ran across the front lawn. Don't worry—neither of the children was your darling daughter Carmelita. They were two replacement orphans for those three Baudelaire brats who caused so much trouble with Coach Genghis. Like all orphans, the two kidnapped brats were so stupid that they didn't even look scared as Ms. K. carried them away. Their faces were very serious, as if they were embarking on an important mission of some kind.

Things are a bit slow at the school without Ms. K. As you recall, our gym teacher, Coach Genghis, no longer teaches here, and Mrs. Bass always seems to be taking a day off to take care of some business she has at the bank. Without any teachers or coaches of any kind, the children have nothing better to do than sit outside and stare glumly at a camera I have placed underneath the immense stone arch printed with our school's motto. On the plus side, however, this leaves me plenty of time to practice the violin.

I am grateful that busy parents such as yourselves took the time to bring the article to my attention. Thank you very much, and please thank Eleanora

Poe for me, if you happen to run into her.

Fairly sincerely,

Vice Principal Nero

Vice Principal Nero

P.S. Enclosed is the list of books Ms. K. was planning to give her students, so you have an idea of how much danger we avoided.

Cleary, Beverly, <u>Ramona Quimby, Age 8</u>

Dahl, Roald, <u>Matilda</u>

Doyle, Vincent Francis, <u>Ivan Lachrymose:</u>
<u>Lake Explorer</u>

Grimm, the Brothers, <u>Grimm's Fairy Tales</u>

Hudson, W.H., <u>Green Mansions</u>

Poe, Edgar Allan, <u>The Coded Poetry of</u>
<u>Edgar Allan Poe</u>

Pukalie, Lena, <u>I Lost Something at the</u>
<u>Movies</u>

Salinger, J.D., <u>Nine Stories</u>

Sir (?), <u>The History of Lucky Smells</u>
<u>Lumbermill</u>

Snicket, Lemony, <u>A Series of Unfortunate</u>
<u>Events</u>

White, E.B., <u>Charlotte's Web</u>

Wilder, Laura Ingalls, <u>Little House in</u>
<u>the Big Woods.</u>

Dear Mr. Funcoot,

Thank you very much for sending me the article that appeared in *The Daily Punctilio.* You were correct in making the assumption that I had not read about the danger of allowing telephone poles to remain upright. The only section of *The Daily Punctilio* I read is the updates on the murder of Count Omar by those three vicious children.

Because of the article you sent me, I have chopped down all of the telephone poles along the street where I live. Thanks to Eleanora Poe, the honest and trustworthy editor-in-chief of *The Daily Punctilio,* and Geraldine Julienne, her star reporter, drivers along Rarely Ridden Road will not be at risk of having a telephone pole suddenly fall on top of them.

I am grateful that a busy playwright such as yourself took the time to bring the article to my attention. Thank you very much, and please thank Eleanora Poe for me, if you happen to run into her.

Reasonably sincerely,

P.S. Enclosed are photographs of some of the telephone poles I chopped down, so you have an idea of how much danger we avoided.

Last night I could not sleep and decided to read the most boring book in my library as a remedy. Imagine my surprise when I found an audio tape wedged between pages 302 and 303. The tape is often noisy, but I managed to transcribe the following conversation.

MAN: (coughing)

WOMAN: Dear me, Arthur. You've had that cough since we were children and it never seems to get better.

MAN: Never mind, Eleanora. Thank you for meeting me for lunch.

WOMAN: It's never a chore to lunch with a sibling, Arthur. And this restaurant seems charming.

MAN: It *is* charming. I was here on official bank business not so long ago and had a very nice lunch, even if one of my companions turned out to be a notorious criminal. Allow me to recommend the Cheer-Up Cheeseburgers.

WOMAN: The Surprising Chicken Salad sounds good, too. Waiter, could you please take our order?

WAITER: I didn't realize this was a sad occasion.

WOMAN: What?

MAN: He keeps saying that. When I was waiting for you to arrive he walked up to me and said the exact same thing.

WOMAN: What is he talking about?

MAN: (coughing)

WAITER: I didn't realize this was a sad occasion.

MAN: Stop saying that! It's not a sad occasion! I'm having lunch with my sister.

WOMAN: Waiter, just please bring us a Cheer-Up Cheeseburger and a Surprising Chicken Salad, and stop your nonsense.

WAITER: I didn't realize—

WOMAN: That's enough from you. What a strange waiter. Now, Arthur, what was this important matter you wanted to discuss?

MAN: (coughing)

WOMAN: We've already discussed your cough.

MAN: No, I was just coughing, Eleanora. What I wanted to discuss is something of an awkward matter. I've been noticing that the coverage by your newspaper of recent events in the Baudelaire case has been somewhat—

WOMAN: Excuse me, Arthur. Sir, why are you holding a microphone near our table?

MAN: I'm *not* holding a micro—

WOMAN: Not you, Arthur. *You*, sir.

WAITER: Me? I didn't realize this was a sad—

WOMAN: Not you either, Waiter. *You*, sir. With the

microphone. *You*, pretending not to hear me. I'm talking to *you*. Turn that microphone off at once!

The tape ends here.

THE OFFICE OF THE VICE PRESIDENT OF ORPHAN AFFAIRS,

MULCTUARY MONEY MANAGEMENT,

"WHERE YOUR MONEY IS COUNTED."

DEAR ELEANORA,

THANK YOU FOR SENDING ME THE ARTICLE WHICH APPEARED IN THE DAILY
PUNCTILIO. YOU WERE CORRECT IN MAKING THE ASSUMPTION THAT I HAD NOT
READ ABOUT THE DANGER OF ALLOWING TELEGRAMS TO BE SENT TO A BANK.
THE ONLY SECTION OF THE DAILY PUNCTILIO I READ IS THE FINANCIAL TIMES.

BECAUSE OF THE ARTICLE YOU SENT ME, I HAVE INSTRUCTED ALL
EMPLOYEES OF MULCTUARY MONEY MANAGEMENT TO IGNORE ANY TELEGRAMS
THAT REACH THE BANK. THANKS TO YOU, MY HONEST AND TRUSTWORTHY
SISTER, AND YOUR STAR REPORTER, GERALDINE JULIENNE, THE VICE
PRESIDENT IN CHARGE OF ORPHAN AFFAIRS WILL ONLY RECEIVE INFORMATION
FROM YOU, AND NOT FROM UNRELIABLE SOURCES.

FINANCIALLY SINCERELY,

Vice President Poe

VICE PRESIDENT POE

P.S. Enclosed are two telegrams I recently ignored, so you have an idea of how much danger we avoided.

P.P.S. Have you heard from you-know-who?

CALL LETTERS   QKC TELEGRAM PD   CHARGE TO

TO: MR. POE AT MULCTUARY MONEY MANAGEME
FROM: VIOLET, KLAUS, AND SUNNY BAUDELAI

PLEASE DO NOT BELIEVE THE STORY
ABOUT US PRINTED IN THE DAILY
PUNCTILIO STOP. COUNT OLAF IS
NOT REALLY DEAD, AND WE DID NOT
REALLY MURDER HI M STOP. SOON
AFTER OUR ARRIVAL IN THE TOWN
121 OF V.F.D., WE WERE INFORMED THAT
COUNT OLAF HAD BEEN CAPTURED
STOP. ALTHOUGH THE ARRESTED MAN
HAD AN EYE TATTOED ON HIS ANKLE
AND ONE EYEBROW INSTEAD OF TWO,
HE WAS NOT COUNT OLAF STOP. HIS

NAME
THE
MURI
IN T
ESME
PLAI
PARI
DIS
AND

SENDI

Send the above message, subject to the terms on back hereo

PLEASE TYPE OR WRITE PLAIN
WU 1269 (R 5-69)

IGNORED

140

QUES SNICKET STOP.
HE WAS FOUND
COUNT OLAF ARRIVED
WITH HIS GIRLFRIEND.
STOP. AS PART OF HIS
L THE FORTUNE OUR
BEHIND, COUNT OLAF
MSELF AS A DETECTIVE
D THE TOWN OF V.F.D.

Telefax
nion
TELEGRAM PD   CHARGE
                   TO

OE AT MULCTUARY MONEY MANGEMENT
ANORA POE AT THE DAILY PUNCTILIO

LP ME, MY DEAR BROTHER STOP. DUE TO
ONS FROM A FAMOUS ACTRESS, MY STAR
HAS LOCKED ME IN THE BASEMENT OF THE
R BUILDING STOP. I AM BEGINNING TO THINK
E OF THE STORIES I HAVE PUBLISHED IN THE
NCTILIO ARE NOT TRUE AFTER ALL STOP. PLEASE
OP. THIS BASEMENT IS FILTHY AND DAMP STOP.

141

SENDING BLANK

Will I ever
see her
again?

142

*What has happened to
the reptiles in
Dr. Montgomery's
collection?*

CHAPTER NINE

~~Why is
Lemony Snicket
on the run?~~

Your Royal Duchessness,

The bell of regret, I'm sorry to say, must ring. Attending your Masked Ball is impossible. Though I'd love to attend your Masked Ball, my enemies are unlikely to cancel their plans—Masked Ball, perhaps, or a Regular Ball or another kind of Ball— of finding and capturing me. Deep, deep, deep, deep regret is what I feel for refusing your invitation, but it's too dangerous. They're searching furiously for the survivors of Dr. Montgomery's collection, but imagine how furiously they'll search for me. So I'll run. I'll hide. I'll run to hiding places. I'll do everything except be at your Masked Ball, even though I'd love to be there.

Maybe next time. I hope so.

With all due respect,

Lemony Snicket

Lemony Snicket

P.S. Ring, bells of regret!

Dear Genius,

Gathering information on Dr. Montgomery's reptile collection, as you requested, is as simple as finding a needle in a haystack, if there were a sign over the haystack reading "Needle Here!" with a brightly colored arrow pointing to the exact location of the needle. Finding the reptiles themselves is as difficult as falling off a log, if the log were so sticky that it was practically impossible to remove oneself from it.

As this was Phase One of my search, I adopted Phase One of Disguise Training: Veiled Facial Disguises. As you can see from the two pictures below, I changed my appearance entirely before embarking on my mission.

With my disguise in place, I went to my local library, which was decorated with a new sign that looked like this:

The World Is at Your Fingertips at the Library! Please Be Quiet Here.

Whistling one of my favorite tunes, I entered the building and found the librarian, an old man with neatly trimmed gray hair and a mustache that turned up at the ends. He was dressed as if everything he wore—a flowered shirt, striped tie, tweed coat, and plaid slacks—had come from different stores or from a rummage sale, except that the crease in his trousers was sharp and his shoes were shined. When I told him I was looking for information on the reptiles in Dr. Montgomery's collection, the old man, whose back was very straight, saluted me as if I were a soldier and said, "Well, young lady, have you been good to your mother?"

"What?" I replied.

"Never mind," he said quickly, and led me to the Children's Room, where to my amazement there was a book all about Dr. Montgomery's collection and three obnoxious children who visited it. The book is called *The Reptile Room,* and I was quickly able to find several passages describing the collection:

From Chapter Two:

There were all sorts of snakes, naturally, but there were also lizards, toads, and assorted other animals that the children had never seen before, not even in pictures, or at the zoo. There was a very fat toad with two wings coming out of its back, and a two-headed lizard that had bright yellow stripes on its belly. There was a snake that had three mouths, one on top of the other, and another that seemed to have no mouth at all. There was a lizard that looked like an owl, with wide eyes that gazed at them from the log on which it was perched in its cage, and a toad that looked just like a church, complete with stained-glass eyes.

From Chapter Three:

. . . the Alaskan Cow Lizard, a long green crea-ture that produced delicious milk. They met the Dissonant Toad, which could imitate human speech in a gravelly voice. Uncle Monty [note: I didn't read the book very carefully, but Uncle Monty seems to be a close friend of Dr. Montgomery's] taught them how to handle the Inky Newt without getting its black dye all over their fingers, and how to tell when the Irascible Python was grumpy and best left alone. He taught them not to give the Green Gimlet Toad too much water, and to never, under any circumstances, let the Virginian Wolfsnake near a typewriter.

From Chapter Thirteen:

"Good-bye, good-bye!" the brilliant Baudelaires called, and waved to Uncle Monty's reptiles. They stood together in the moonlight, and kept waving, even when Bruce shut the doors of the van, even as the van drove past the snake-shaped hedges and down the driveway to Lousy Lane, and even when it turned a corner and disappeared into the dark.

Unfortunately, the book ends soon afterward, and the author does not say what happened to Uncle Monty's reptiles after the reptiles stood together in the moonlight and kept waving. The author does not even explain how the reptiles were able to wave at all—particularly the snakes, who have no hands.

I was ready to embark on Phase Two, and disguised myself accordingly:

Due to the nature of my disguise, I had to conduct my investigation in a somewhat wandering fashion, best described with the following map.

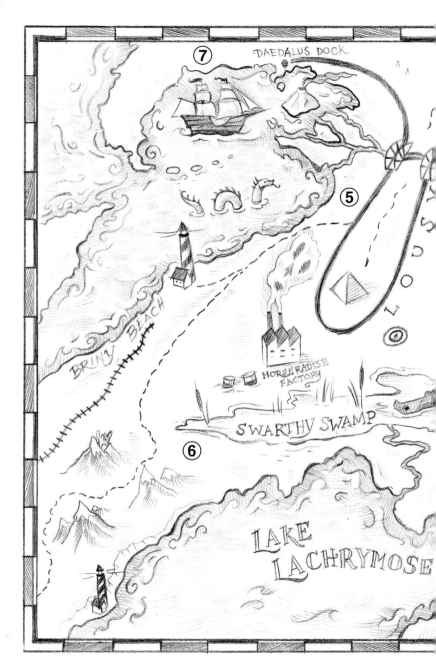

① Approached this supposed house of worship to determine if it was actually "a toad that looked just like a church, complete with stained-glass eyes," as described in Chapter Two. Building did not move—proving either that it is actually a church and not a toad, or that the toad is very large, and sleeps very soundly.

② Overheard a gravelly voice, as in "the Dissonant Toad, which could imitate human speech in a gravelly voice," described in Chapter Three. I hid behind a tree in order to disguise myself as a cow, hiding behind a tree. The voice was muttering, apparently to itself, on how inconvenient it was to drown someone, because it got all wet and it hated that. Concluded it was not a toad because toads like to get wet.

③ Lovely wildflowers located here. Took a break to smell them.

④ Observed a black snake, possibly the Mamba du Mal, appearing to communicate with several crickets. Accidentally mooed and frightened everyone away.

⑤ Spotted yellow stripes, as in "a two-headed lizard that had bright yellow stripes on its belly," as described in Chapter Two. Yellow stripes were discovered to be made of paint, placed in the center of Lousy Lane to divide traffic.

⑥ Eavesdropped on a picnic. Child telling its mother that it saw a fat toad with two wings coming out of its back, as described in Chapter Two. Mother telling its child not to be silly. Child telling its mother it wasn't being silly. Mother telling its child of course it was. Child telling its mother it was not. Mother saying was so. Child saying was not. Mother saying was so. Child saying was not. Mother saying was so. Grew bored, wandered off.

⑦ Approached a married couple who apparently own the *Prospero* to ask if any reptiles had recently boarded the ship. Couple, alarmed by talking cow, refused to participate.

⑧ Saw signs indicating there was a dairy nearby. Did not approach due to fear of being milked.

With all due respect,

NOTE TO FILE:

The library at Prufrock Preparatory School was a pleasant place, with comfortable chairs, huge wooden bookshelves, brass lamps in the shapes of different fish, and bright blue curtains that rippled like water as a breeze came in from the window. The librarian was an old man with neatly trimmed gray hair and a mustache that turned up at the ends. He was dressed as if everything he wore—a flowered shirt, striped tie, tweed coat, and plaid slacks—had come from different stores or from a rummage sale, except that the crease in his trousers was sharp and his shoes were shined.

As soon as I began to sing the coded song, the old man, whose back was very straight, saluted me as if I were a soldier and said, "Well, young lady, have you been good to your mother?" a phrase which here means "I have a message for you." I gave the coded reply—"The question is, has she been good to me?"—and received the following note in return:

Dear Mr. Snicket,

We realize it is risky to write to you, but we thought you should know that one of O's henchmen, disguised as a cow, approached us asking about Dr. Montgomery's reptiles.

Don't worry — we did not mention anything concerning our assistance with the Incredibly Deadly Viper — but we fear that the henchman could use his disguise to cause trouble at Valorous Farms Dairy.

"The world is quiet here."

156

CHAPTER TEN

~~How many associates does Count Olaf have?~~

What can be hidden
in a book?

Dear Dairy,

For obvious reasons, I never told you about my note-book, with a cover as green as mansions long gone, which I use as a commonplace book, a phrase which here means "place where I have collected passages from some of the most important books I have read." These passages hold some of the most crucial secrets in this sad and flammable world. As much as it breaks my heart to tear them from my dark green notebook, it is simply not safe to keep them any longer.

With all due respect,

Lemony Snicket

Lemony Snicket

NOTE:

For various reasons, portions of this chapter have been changed or made up entirely, including this sentence.

out.
wailing
s of his theater
into the kitchen. Soon they were
crowding the room—an assortment of strange-
looking characters of all shapes and sizes. There
was a bald man with a very long nose, dressed
in a long black robe. There were two women
who had bright white powder all over their
faces, making them look like ghosts. Behind the
women was a man with very long and skinny
arms, at the end of which were two hooks
instead of hands. There was a person who was
extremely fat, and who looked like neither a

man nor a woman. And behind this person,
standing in the doorway, were an assortment of
people the children could not see but who
promised to be just as frightening.

Lemony Snicket, The Bad
Beginning (HarperCollins, 1999),
pp. 47-48.

Chapter 6

Ivan Lachrymose
Has a Snack

LATER that day, Ivan Lachrymose was feeling hungry and decided to have a snack. "I'm feeling hungry," he said. "I think I'll have a snack." He left his bedroom, where he had been making his bed, and walked down the hallway. At the end of the hallway was a door. He opened the door and walked through it into the kitchen. "Here I am in the kitchen," he said, "the perfect place to find a snack. I'll open the first cupboard and see if it contains a good snack." He opened the first cupboard. It contained wheat flour. "I don't want to eat wheat flour for a snack," he said. "I'll open the second cupboard and see if it contains a good snack." He opened the second cupboard. It contained cornmeal. "I don't want to eat cornmeal for a snack," he said. "I'll open the third cupboard and see if it contains a good snack." It contained molasses. At this point, I hope this book is so boring that no one is reading it, because this tedious biography was not written for people to read. It was written so that crucial documents could be stored right here, between pages 302 and 303. If, by any chance, you are reading this book for

302

entertainment and not to find crucial documents, allow me to apologize for how boring it is. "I don't want to eat molasses for a snack," he said. "I'll open the fourth cupboard and see if it contains a good snack."

Vincent Francis Doyle, Ivan Lachrymose: Lake Explorer (Very False Documents Press), pp. 302 - 303.

162

when the tune came to an end, she turned
around and found herself face to face
with an old man with neatly trimmed
gray hair and a moustache that turned up
at the ends. He was dressed as if everything
he wore--a flowered shirt, striped tie,
tweed coat, and plaid slacks--had come from
different stores or from a rummage sale,
except that the crease in his trousers
was sharp and his shoes were shined.
     The old man, whose back was very straight,
saluted Ramona as if she were a soldier
and said, "Well, young lady, have you been
good to your mother?"

Beverly Cleary, Ramona Quimby, Age 8
(Harper Trophy, 1992), pp. 177-178.

PHOTO HIGHLIGHTS FROM LAST YEAR'S
IN AUCTION (*cont.*):

The Esmé Squalor Fan Club proudly displays the Mambu du Mal.

The famous snake was formerly owned by

Dr. Montgomery Montgomery, who died in an accident

as reported in *The Daily Punctilio*.

Now dead and attractively displayed in a frame,

the snake was bid on by several unidentified sources.

These lucky ladies were the winners!

The In Auction Catalog (Very Fancy Daily Press), p. 78.

Zombies in the Snow is such a strange film, with such awkward dialogue, that one wonders if it is meant to be a piece of entertainment at all, but instead some sort of coded message. Th...

Lena Pukalie, I Lost Something at the Movies (Voracious Film Discussions Press), pp. 302-303.

Klaus walked over to the stack of books and opened the one on top. He had marked his place with a small piece of paper, so he found what he was looking for right away. "'The Mamba du Mal,'" he read out loud, "'is one of the deadliest snakes in the hemisphere, noted for its strangulatory grip, used in conjunction with its deadly venom, giving all of its victims a tenebrous hue, which is ghastly to behold.'" He put the book down, and turned to Mr. Poe.

Lemony Snichet *The Reptile Room* (HarperCollins, 1999) p. 169.

The Mamba du Mal is one of the deadliest snakes in the hemisphere, noted for its strangulatory grip, used in conjunction with its deadly venom, giving all of its victims a tenebrous hue, which is ghastly to behold. More pleasant to contemplate, however, are the snake's excellent communication skills. Certain specimens of the Mamba du Mal have been trained to recite certain phrases in an encoded form of English so they might be employed as guardians of crucial headquarters. A Mamba du Mal hissing the phrase "Summer is" for instance, is communicating a coded version of the phrase "Enemies are nearby." The hissed phrase "over and gone" translates to "probably in disguise," and the Mamba has been known to hiss the word "dying" as a code for "Beware of arson." The only other creature with communication skills sufficient to convey these messages is the common grass cricket.

Tony "Mommy" Eggmonterol, The Mamba du Mal: A Snake That Will Never Kill Me (Venom Feels Delightful Press) p.169.

There once lived in ~~a town~~ an old Count, who had just one son: but he was as dimwitted as a baby yak, and could learn nothing. So his father said to him: "Listen to me, my dimwitted son. I can get nothing into your head, no matter how hard I try. You must go far away from here, and study with a renowned Professor in a large city for one year."

At the end of the year the son returned home, and his father asked: "Dimwitted son, what have you learnt?"

"Father, I have learnt the language of dogs."

"A curse on your dimwitted head!" cried his father, "is that all you have learnt? I will send you to another Professor in the suburbs." The youth was taken there, and remained with this Professor for another year.

When the son returned his father asked him again: "Dimwitted offspring, what have you learnt?"

He answered: "I have learnt bird language."

Then the father threw a wild tantrum, and roared: "Dimwitted fruit of my loins, have you learnt nothing all this time? Aren't you ashamed to come into my presence? I will send you to study with a third Professor in the hinterlands, but if you learn nothing this time, I won't be your father any longer."

The son stayed with the third Professor for one more year, and when he came home again and his father asked, "My dimwitted hobbledehoy, what have you learnt?"

He answered, "I have learnt the cricket language."

The Brothers Grimm, "The Three Languages," from Grimm's Fairy Tales, (Märchen Press), pp. 2, 3, 6

ɪ ᴏᴠ.

At night, when Laura lay awake in the
rundle bed, she listened and could not hear
nything at all but the sound of the trees whis-
ering together. Sometimes, far away in the
night, a wolf howled. Then he came nearer,
and howled again.

Laura Ingalls Wilder, Little House
in the Big Woods (Harper Trophy
1994), p. 3, found tangled in the
branches of Nevermore Tree.

It happens to be wedding I'd give
a lot to be able to get to and when
the invitation first arrived, I thought
it might ̶k̶a̶x̶x̶ just be possible for me to
make the trip...

J. D. Salinger "For Esmé With Love
and Squalor," from Nine Stories,
(Little, Brown, 1954, 2001), p. 87.

169

Hear the mellow wedding bells—
Golden bells!
What a world of happiness their harmony
foretells!

Edgar Allan Poe, "The Bells," from *The Coded Poetry of Edgar Allan Poe*, p. 495

Our special "emerald lumber" was used for
years by a variety of organizations for the
construction of their green headq**uarters** and
for a few green homes, including the mansions
constructed by the Snicket, Quagmire, and
Baudelaire families.

Sir, *The History of Lucky Smells Lumbermill*

The librarian at my school, where I was the smartest person in the whole wide world, was an old man with neatly trimmed gray hair and a moustache that turned up at the ends. He was dressed as if everything he wore—a flowered shirt, striped tie, tweed coat, and plaid slacks—had come from different stores or from a rummage sale, except that the crease in his trousers was sharp and his shoes were shined.

One day, the old man, whose back was very straight, saluted me as if I were a soldier and said, "Well, young lady, have you been good to your mother?"

"Go away, creep," I replied. "Your n

Carmelita Spats, *Me: The Completely Authorized Autobiography of the Prettiest, Smartest, Most Darling Girl in the Whole Wide World* (Spoiled Brat Press), p. 793.

XV. The Crickets

THE CRICKETS sang in the grasses. They sang the song of summer's ending, a sad, monotonous song. "Summer is over and gone," they sang. "Over and gone, over and gone. Summer is dying, dying."

The crickets felt it was their duty to warn everybody that summertime cannot last forever. Even on the most beautiful days in the whole year—the days when summer is changing into fall—the crickets spread the rumor of sadness and change.

E.B. White, Charlotte's Web (Harper Trophy, 1999) p. 113.

It is a cause of very great regret to me that
this task has taken so much longer a time
than I had e xpected for its completion....
A darkened chamber, the existence of which
had never been suspected in that familiar
house... furnished only with an ebony stand
...its surface ornamented with flower and
leaf and thorn, and winding through it all the
figure of a serpent;...and finally, the disposal of the mysterious ashes--that was all
there was relating to an untold chapter in a
man's life for imagination to work on.

W. H. Hudson, _Green Mansions_,
(S. Little + Ives Company, 1904), p. 9.

_Hear the loud alarum bells—
Brazen bells!
What tale of terror, now, their turbulency
tells!_

Edgar Allan Poe, "The Bells" from
_The Coded Poetry of Edgar Allan
Poe_, p. 495.

"How I love the sound of bells!" the littlest elf said to his new friends in the forest. "They're so ringy."

"Of course they're ringy," replied the snake in a bored tone. "They're bells."

Monty Kensiel, The Littlest Elf.
p. 7½.

bald men w/ long nose   1
powder-faced women   2
hook-handed man   1
person of unknown gender
        and great girth   1
assortment of people the children
        could not see   7?
Ivan Lachrymose   1
Esmé Squalor Fan Club   14

(+ who took photo?)
"Enemies are nearby"   6?
old Count   1
an only son   1
professors   3
Lena Pukalie   1?
"a man's life"   1?

Grand total of Olaf's associates
as recorded in commonplace
        book to date:

        at least   (25)
        possibly more than (41)

Hal,

Please place the enclosed papers in the Baudelaire file even though they are marked Snicket. They appear to be various attempts to compose an opening sentence for a rather gruesome-sounding children's book.

With all due respect,

Babs

Babs

My life story, like most people's, begins when I was very young.

Once upon a time, there was a young man who was whisked away from his family in order to join a noble organization. Or so I thought.

What follows is a story so depressing it is no wonder *The Daily Punctilio* did not report it correctly.

Don't read this.

I wish this book could begin: Once upon a time, after a confusing if exciting childhood, I met a woman, fell in love, and lived happily ever after.

Once upon a time, after a confusing if exciting childhood, I met a woman, fell in love, and was never happy again.

Many years after my life took an unfortunate turn, three children took a trip to Briny Beach.

I am weeping as I write this, and soon you will be weeping as you read it.

Perhaps one day you heard a noise outside your home, and your parents told you it was nothing.

Please don't read this.

If you are interested in stories with happy endings, go away.

If you are interested in stories with happy endings, boy are you in trouble.

If you are interested in stories with happy endings, you would be better off reading some other book.

CHAPTER ELEVEN

Why do so many things end in fire?

~~Are the Baudelaire~~

~~parents really dead?~~

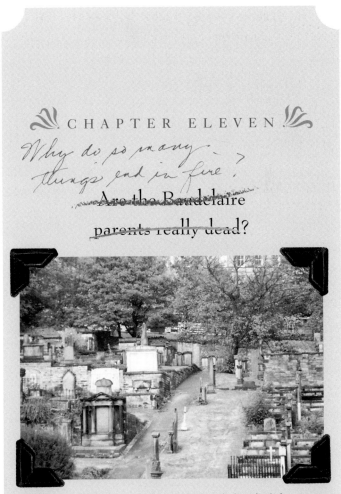

Note: the Baudelaires are not buried here.

Or here.

HELQUIST ARTIST SERVICES

Dear Mr. Snicket,

I am very sorry to report that I arrived too late to make any sketches that might clear your name or provide any information on the survivor or survivors you think may exist. By the time the Official Fire Department allowed me to view the scene, the entire building was more or less destroyed. I tried to sit for a moment and draw some of the objects that lay in the rubble—a glass bottle, portions of a grand piano, a few charred pieces of green wood, the remains of a tea set—but the smoke overwhelmed me and I had to walk across the street, where I made the enclosed drawing.

   The Daily Punctilio has never seemed like a reliable paper, and I shudder to think how they will report this terrible tragedy. I never believed the stories I read about you, Mr. Snicket, in relation to the Quagmire case or any other. I look forward to meeting with you to discuss how my illustrative skills can be of any assistance in bringing the truth to the general public.

See you at the dairy. So many stories have ended in fire, Mr. Snicket. Let's hope this one ends differently.

With all due respect,

Brett Helquist

DAIRY BURNS DOWN

The Valorous Farms Dairy burned down late last night during a heavy thunderstorm. Detective Smith, arriving on the scene, described the fire as an accident, dismissing rumors that a cow had been seen lurking suspiciously in the surrounding area. "Another case solved without any help from volunteers," he commented. Reporters from *The Daily Punctilio* were not allowed to view the location, but Detective Smith provided this illustration for our readers. "The drawing was found in a pile of papers which survived the fire," Smith explained. "I assume that someone was drawing the fire during the fire."

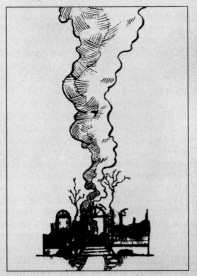

NOTE TO FILE:

This photograph of the Valorous Farms Dairy was taken by Meredith Heuer, who apologizes for the blurriness caused by the previous evening's thunderstorm.

CHAPTER TWELVE

*If there's nothing out
there what was that noise?*

~~Is there anything a
concerned citizen can do
if he or she wants to
help the Baudelaires?~~

INFREQUENTLY ASKED QUESTIONS ABOUT V.F.D.

I. HOW DO I VOLUNTEER FOR YOUR ORGANIZATION?

Since the schism, it has become much more difficult for our members to contact possible volunteers. It is possible you've been contacted about possible membership already but did not notice. Perhaps a waiter said something strange to you in a restaurant. Perhaps a librarian asked you a question concerning your mother, or your mother asked you a question concerning your librarian. Perhaps your teacher gave you a list of books that had coded messages inside, or perhaps you detected a message in a newspaper you found blowing around your neighborhood. Perhaps a taxi driver showed you a photograph of people you did not know, or perhaps you looked at a photograph of yourself and saw people you did not recognize in the background. Perhaps a bullfighter approached you with a telegram, or perhaps a chest of drawers whispered something when you thought you were alone, or perhaps you were aboard a ship, an airplane, a bus, or an automobile that departed early, late, or exactly on time.

If you think you have been contacted and are interested in volunteering, you may want to keep a commonplace book, which is a notebook where you can copy parts of books you think are in code, or take notes on a series of events you may have observed that are suspicious, unfortunate, or very dull. Keep your commonplace book in a safe place, such as underneath your bed, or at a nearby dairy.

2. HOW DOES MY VOLUNTEERING BEGIN?

On the day you officially join the organization, you will hear a noise outside your home. It may sound like the howl of a wolf, the cawing of a crow, the hissing of a snake, the chirping of a cricket, the engine of an automobile, the keys of a typewriter, the striking of a match, or the turning of a page. The noise will come in the middle of the night, the middle of the morning, or, in very rare cases, late in the afternoon. Ask your parents what the noise was. If they reply "nothing," they are replying in code, because there is never "nothing" outside one's home. If you are interested in volunteering, answer your parents with the following question: "If there's nothing out there, what was that noise?" We will be listening, and will know it is safe to act.

Note: If you have no parents, we'll contact you in a more direct manner.

3. DO I HAVE TO GET A TATTOO?

Not anymore. Since the schism, we have realized that it is not wise to permanently mark oneself with a symbol when the meaning of the symbol may change at any moment.

4. HOW LONG WILL IT BE BEFORE I SEE MY PARENTS AGAIN?

My dear sister,
  I understand how
desperate our situation
has become, but it is
dreadful enough for people
to have to read about the
Baudelaires. I cannot
imagine who would be
brave enough to help them.
  With all due respect,
    Lemony Snicket

There was a long pause, and I realized this curious stranger was at last done telling this confusing and unnerving story. Without another word the storyteller handed me this packet of material, which I give to you now.

~~who is~~
who is

~~Lemony Snicket?~~ ?

~~...~~
~~...~~

𝓐.

𝓑.

𝓒.

𝓐.	whereabouts unknown
𝓑.	whereabouts uninteresting
𝓒.	Chas. Snicket

the family Tree

volunteer

Great(?) Britain

I arrived too late--they'd already removed it.

turned out there was a floor above the penthouse.

202

...did not stop weeping for nine days.

...could not possibly have been at the same time

Very fast delivery

..could not possibly have been at the same time.

After the schism,

I thought one of the cars was behaving strangely

209

If there's nothing out there,

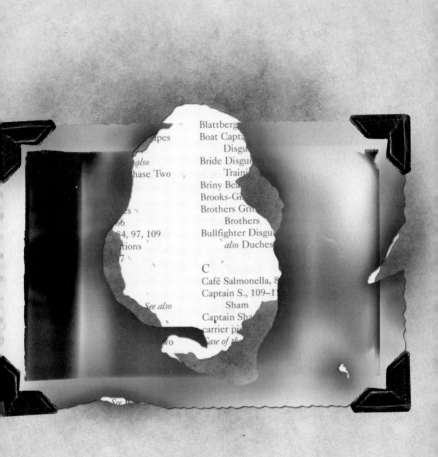

Index

R

S

T